BITTER RIVALS

Amy turned on Enid, her voice caustic. "Enid Rollins," she said, her eyes flashing fire, "didn't I tell you before just to get lost? Don't you ho......

...ns won't ever talk to you again after tonight. And neither will Liz!"

Bantam Books in the Sweet Valley High Series
Ask your bookseller for the books you have missed

SWEET VALLEY HIGH

BITTER RIVALS

Written by
Kate William

Created by
FRANCINE PASCAL

BANTAM BOOKS
TORONTO • NEW YORK • LONDON • SYDNEY • AUCKLAND

RL6, IL age 12 and up

BITTER RIVALS
A Bantam Book / July 1986

Sweet Valley High is a trademark of Francine Pascal

Conceived by Francine Pascal

*Produced by Cloverdale Press, Inc.
133 Fifth Avenue, New York, N.Y. 10003*

Cover art by James Mathewuse.

ISBN 0-553-25728-5

Published simultaneously in the United States and Canada

Bantam Books are published by Bantam Books, Inc. Its trademark, consisting
of the words "Bantam Books" and the portrayal of a rooster, is Registered in
U.S. Patent and Trademark Office and in other countries. Marca Registrada.
Bantam Books, Inc., 666 Fifth Avenue, New York, New York 10103.

PRINTED IN THE UNITED STATES OF AMERICA

O   12 11 10 9 8 7 6 5

BITTER
RIVALS

One

"Elizabeth, you're not even listening to me!" Jessica Wakefield complained as she sat dangling her slender, tan legs in the shallow end of the Wakefields' swimming pool. It was Friday afternoon, and the twins were relaxing in the sun with Elizabeth's best friend, Enid Rollins, who had just joined them. Elizabeth thought the world of her friend and was delighted Enid had come over. But she knew her twin disagreed.

It might have been hard for a stranger to believe that Elizabeth and Jessica Wakefield could disagree about anything. As far as appearances went, they were identical—from their silky, sun-streaked blond hair and blue-green eyes to the tiny dimple each showed when she smiled. Both girls were five feet six inches tall and a perfect size six. Slender, willowy, blond described the Wakefield twins to a T.

But anyone who knew the twins rarely mixed them up. That wasn't just because Elizabeth wore a wristwatch and Jessica, who operated by

1

what her parents teasingly called "Jessica Standard Time," never did. Ned Wakefield, the twins' father, often joked that not even years of legal training had prepared him for the baffling case of these identical opposites.

Each twin had a completely different sense of style. Elizabeth liked tailored clothes—neat skirts and sweaters, chinos, polo shirts—clothing she knew would stay in style for years. Jessica, on the other hand, bought the latest things and usually got sick of them before they became unfashionable. Elizabeth had known for years what she wanted to be when she grew up. She wanted to be a writer, and she devoted a great deal of time writing articles as well as the "Eyes and Ears" column for *The Oracle*, the student newspaper at Sweet Valley High, the school the twins attended. Jessica's interests seemed to change every week. First it was acting, then dancing, then the very briefest stint at the twins' father's law office, fueled by one of Jessica's crushes. Jessica's motto was to have a good time, no matter what. She was as impatient and excitable as her twin was calm and steady. And just then it looked as if Jessica was going to explode if she couldn't get her sister's attention.

"Liz," she said again, splashing some water from the pool up onto her twin's legs. Elizabeth was sitting beside her, but from the dreamy expression on her face, she might as well have been a million miles away. "Hey!" Jessica giggled, leaning over and pretending to tap her sister's forehead. "Anyone home there?"

Elizabeth broke into a smile, her turquoise eyes crinkling up at the corners. "Sorry, Jess," she said. "I was just thinking about Amy Sutton, that's all. I can't believe she's really moving back to Sweet Valley!"

Enid's green eyes looked thoughtful as she ran her slender hand through the water. "When are they moving in, Liz? Do you know yet?"

Elizabeth shook her head. "Amy called last night, but she still didn't have a very clear idea of when it'll be. It sounds as though it could be any time, though." She hugged her knees with excitement. "I can't believe it! Enid, I can't wait for you to meet each other."

Enid smiled, looking down at the water. "I just hope we like each other," she said. "I mean—"

"Enid Rollins!" Elizabeth exclaimed with mock horror, jumping up and running over to hug her friend. "Of *course* you'll like each other! Amy Sutton is fabulous. She's so vivacious, so bouncy, so much fun—"

"You make her sound like a trampoline," Jessica cut in.

Jessica wasn't anywhere near as excited as Elizabeth about Amy Sutton's arrival. Jessica hadn't known Amy as well as her twin. Elizabeth and Amy had been inseparable for years, right up till the day Amy moved away, after sixth grade. Jessica remembered how heartbroken her sister had been. She wondered if Amy had changed very much during the past five years. She also wondered, looking slyly at Enid out of the corner of her eye, what Amy's arrival was going to mean to the apparently unshakable devotion between Elizabeth and Enid. It seemed to Jessica that Enid looked less than thrilled at the prospect of meeting the much-talked-about Amy Sutton, and personally Jessica didn't blame her. *When you're as big a wimp as Enid Rollins*, she thought meanly, *why look forward to meeting someone vivacious and fun?*

"She said last night that when they move depends on her mother," Elizabeth went on. "Mrs. Sutton's contract with the TV station in Connecticut calls for a certain number of sportscasts. She may have to stay on an extra week or two if she can't convince them to let her go."

"It's so exciting," Jessica said, "having a friend whose mother is a real live sportscaster. Do you think she'll be able to introduce us to all sorts of famous athletes?"

"I doubt it," Elizabeth said reprovingly. "Besides, from what Amy says, it sounds as if Mrs. Sutton is busier and busier these days. We'll probably barely get to talk to *her*, let alone to the athletes she interviews."

Amy's mother, Dyan Sutton, was the reason the Sutton family had moved to Connecticut. She had been offered a spot as the main sportscaster on a local TV network, and it seemed too good an opportunity to pass up. Especially as Mr. Sutton was a freelance photographer, and, as he put it, his work was easily transportable. Elizabeth still remembered how horrible it had been, having to say goodbye to Amy. Once Amy moved, it really wasn't the same. At first they had written every week, but gradually the frequency of the letters dwindled. Amy came back to Sweet Valley once or twice and Elizabeth went to Connecticut one Christmas vacation for a visit, but as the years passed, such opportunities decreased. When Elizabeth received a letter from Amy the previous week, she knew something big was up. But she had never in a million years expected the news Amy had sent. The Suttons were coming back to Sweet Valley in just a matter of weeks! Dyan Sutton had been offered a spot on WXAB, close to Sweet Valley. And the Suttons were buying the Bradleys' house, just four blocks away from the Wakefields! Elizabeth had practically flipped, she was so excited.

"Well, I still think it's exciting," Jessica said, grabbing a bottle of suntan oil and squeezing a few drops onto her legs. "It almost makes up for Helen Bradley moving away and deserting the cheerleaders."

Elizabeth laughed. "She's hardly moving just to spite you, Jess. Besides, she's not moving that far, just to Los Angeles. You'll still be able to see her."

Jessica frowned. "That isn't the point, Liz. I

don't really care whether I see her or not. I just don't want to have to deal with auditioning people for her place on the squad, that's all. Remember what happened last time?"

Elizabeth and Enid exchanged glances. They *did* remember! Who could forget? Jessica was co-captain of the squad, but the last time auditions were held, she took charge of the whole show. Annie Whitman had auditioned, and Jessica hadn't wanted Annie on the squad, so she had done her best to keep her off. When Annie found out she hadn't made the squad, she had tried to commit suicide. It had been a terrible mess. Eventually Jessica had had to relent, and now Annie was one of the cheerleaders.

"Nothing like that had better happen this time," Jessica grumbled, putting the suntan oil down and picking up her notebook.

Enid's eyebrows lifted. "Homework? On a Friday afternoon?"

Jessica sounded indignant. "Don't think you two are the only ones interested in literary life around here! It just so happens," she added, flipping her hair back over one shoulder, "that Cara Walker and I are editing our *own* column for *The Oracle*. What do you think of that?"

Elizabeth had found out the previous week about her sister's column, both from Jessica herself and from Penny Ayala, the editor-in-chief of *The Oracle*. But Enid looked surprised. She couldn't help admiring Jessica's energy, though.

Recently Jessica had organized a rocking-chair marathon to raise money for the cheerleaders.

"You? And Cara? What kind of column?" she asked, obviously having a hard time envisioning Jessica and Cara Walker as editorial types. Cara Walker, who was on the cheerleading squad with Jessica and who dated the twins' older brother Steven, was better known for being a good dancer and a lot of fun at parties than for literary talent.

"It's called 'Dear Miss Lovelorn,' " Jessica said proudly. "Cara and I are splitting the work—reading and choosing letters to print and writing answers to them. And believe me, Enid, it's going to be the best thing to hit *The Oracle* in ages."

Enid looked curiously at Jessica's notebook. "Have you gotten any letters yet?"

"Just a few," Jessica admitted, opening her notebook. "But we just announced it last week, and we didn't get the box set up in the *Oracle* office until Monday. Once it gets going, we're going to have millions. Just wait and see."

Elizabeth grinned. "Penny's absolutely thrilled with the idea, Jess. She thinks it's going to be wonderful."

Jessica's eyes sparkled. "Personally," she said, smiling, "I think she's right. After all, who could possibly be in a better situation to offer love advice than yours truly?"

7

"You've got a point there," Enid said wryly. "If you haven't been through it, no one has."

"Come on, Jess," Elizabeth pleaded. "Let's hear one of your inspired responses. I want to know what kind of advice you're giving before I see it in print next week."

"OK," Jessica said, clearing her throat. "Here's the first one Cara and I have done. The letter's from 'A Sad Sophomore' who says: 'Dear Miss Lovelorn, I hate to be one of the first to ask you for advice, but I'm really up a creek. All of my friends have boyfriends except for me. Everywhere I go I seem to be the only one without a date. I'm not sure what I'm doing wrong, since I'm OK-looking and have a decent personality. Can you rush me some advice before I spend the rest of my high school years alone?' "

"Wow," Enid said, looking at Elizabeth. "Serious stuff. What's your response, Jess?"

Jessica cleared her throat again. " 'Dear Sad Sophomore,' " she read back. " 'Quit sulking and start doing the asking yourself. Next time you want a date somewhere, ask someone! And if he says no, go by yourself and have a good time. Miss Lovelorn *always* has fun when she goes places by herself.' "

"Not bad," Elizabeth said, intrigued. "Let's hear another."

"Well, just one more," Jessica told her. "Otherwise, you won't want to read our column next week." She riffled through her papers until she found the one she was looking for. " 'Dear Miss Lovelorn,' " she read. " 'My problem is too many girls! Girls are always fighting over me, and I have ten times as many as I can handle. I can't do anything without getting chased. The thing is that I really am a deep, sensitive guy, and I want a lasting relationship. How can I convince these girls that I want something more?' " Jessica giggled. "Signed, 'Sweet Valley Swinger.' "

Enid burst out laughing. "That one sounds like Bruce Patman," she said. "Or at least, how Bruce *used* to sound. Doesn't it?"

Even Jessica laughed. Bruce Patman was one of the richest young men in Sweet Valley. A senior at Sweet Valley High, he was known for having an ego a mile high, demonstrated by the license plates on his black Porsche: 1BRUCE1. Actually Bruce had changed since he had fallen in love with beautiful Regina Morrow. But the girls were still amused.

"What does Miss Lovelorn say to that?" Elizabeth asked.

Jessica looked back down at the paper. " 'Dear Swinger,' " she read. " 'Miss Lovelorn is unimpressed. You sound like a giant zip in the sincerity department. Any girl worth lasting with will probably stay miles away. Shape up or find another branch to swing from.' "

Enid laughed. "That's pretty good," she

admitted, shaking her head approvingly. "You and Cara sure told him!"

The telephone rang from inside the Wakefields' house, and Elizabeth cocked her ear, listening. "Who's going to get the phone—Miss Lovelorn or me?"

"Miss Lovelorn thinks her darling twin will get it," Jessica said with a lazy smile. She broke into a giggle when she saw the look Elizabeth shot her before dashing into the house.

It was the perfect end to a perfect week, and all Jessica wanted was to sneak in a little nap so she would be perfectly rested for the Beach Disco that night.

That, she thought sleepily, putting her notebook aside and lying down, was *one* good thing about Enid Rollins. You never had to worry about her keeping you awake!

"That was Amy again," Elizabeth told Enid, taking a pitcher of iced tea out of the refrigerator and pouring them each a tall glassful.

"What's up?" Enid asked, taking a sip of tea.

"She just wanted to let me know that she's pretty sure they'll be coming a week from Sunday. Her mom managed to get out of the last two or three shows without offending anyone."

Enid blinked. A week from Sunday. Somehow that seemed so soon—almost *too* soon. "Hey," she said, trying to keep her voice natural, "we still have to figure out what we're going to do about our ski trip, right?''

Elizabeth's face brightened. ''That's right,'' she said, plopping down at the kitchen table. She and Enid had been looking forward to the trip for ages. Enid's Aunt Nancy had a cabin up in the mountains near Lake Tahoe, and she had been urging Enid to come up one weekend and bring a friend. Enid naturally wanted Elizabeth to come along, and Elizabeth thought it sounded like a terrific idea. Nancy was only twenty-eight, and being with her was like having an older sister. She was a bright, perky redhead with a great sense of humor, and Elizabeth was certain the weekend would be fabulous.

Suddenly her face darkened. They had decided, after a great deal of deliberation, that the next weekend was the best time to go. All they had to do was call Enid's aunt and confirm it.

But Elizabeth had just realized that going away that weekend would prevent her from seeing the Suttons when they arrived. Amy thought they were coming Sunday, and Elizabeth really wanted to be home then. She couldn't imagine not being there to welcome her friend back after so many years!

Her cheeks reddening a little, Elizabeth told Enid about her conflict. ''Do you think we could put the trip off for a few weeks?'' she asked

11

uncertainly. "That way there couldn't be a chance of missing Amy when she moves in."

Enid hesitated before answering. "OK," she said at last, making an effort to look as if she didn't mind. "Maybe we can invite Amy to come along when we finally go," she added, ignoring the lump in her throat.

"Enid Rollins, you are the best friend in the whole world," Elizabeth exclaimed. "Not to mention the most understanding person I've ever met. Are you sure your aunt won't mind?"

Enid smiled, though with difficulty . "The good thing about Aunt Nancy is that she's changed plans quite a few times herself. I'm sure she'll understand, Liz. Why don't I just tell her that we'll call her back next week and let her know for sure?"

Elizabeth's aqua eyes shone. "I mean it, Enid," she said again. "I can't tell you how lucky I feel having you for a friend."

Enid bit her lip, saying nothing. She wished she felt a little more enthusiastic about Amy Sutton's arrival.

Two

"OK, Elizabeth Wakefield," Winston Egbert said, facing her across the lunchroom table, "what's this story I've been hearing about the woman of my dreams moving back to Sweet Valley?"

Elizabeth laughed. Winston had a reputation among the members of the junior class as the clown of Sweet Valley High, and she could always count on him for a wisecrack. "It's Amy Sutton," she told him. "You remember her, Winston. And it's true," she added, turning to the others at the table. "She's moving back to Sweet Valley. In fact, her parents have bought Helen Bradley's house."

Lila Fowler, who had already heard the news of Amy's arrival, looked disdainfully at Elizabeth. Pretty, spoiled, and unbelievably wealthy, Lila usually seemed bored. And she didn't look excited at the prospect of Amy's arrival. "Wasn't she kind of clumsy and tomboyish?" she asked, making it sound as though Amy were to be avoided at all costs.

"She wasn't all that clumsy," Elizabeth retorted. "And, yes, she loves sports, all kinds of sports. She's a lot of fun, Lila."

"You don't have to sell *me* on the idea," Winston said, grinning. "We'll have the welcome wagon ready."

Jessica looked up from the pile of letters she was supposed to be sorting through. "Speaking of visitors from faraway places, Lila, whatever happened to that cousin of yours? Wasn't he supposed to be rolling into town one of these days?"

Lila lifted her perfectly shaped eyebrows. "Jess," she purred, "are you trying to suggest that I've been giving you false information? *Of course* Christopher is coming to town. As a matter of fact, I got a call from him this morning. He's coming for three whole weeks—and I intend to spend every minute celebrating."

"Christopher?" DeeDee Gordon said blankly, looking questioningly across the table at Bill Chase, her boyfriend. "Who's Christopher?"

Lila's look was devastating. "Christopher," she said pompously, "is quite simply the world's most fabulous man."

"Lila's cousin," Jessica put in.

Lila smiled. "He's from a really interesting branch of the family tree."

14

Winston laughed. "As opposed to the Fowler trunk, that is," he said teasingly.

Lila ignored him. "And," she went on, "he's six foot two, with really wavy, thick, blond hair, and the most amazing blue eyes. They just sort of pierce right through you."

Enid giggled. "*When* is this gorgeous man coming? Sounds like I should enter that day on my calendar."

Lila prodded her chicken salad with her fork. "He said he's coming this weekend. Christopher doesn't really like being confined to one particular *day*, you see."

"Where did you say he was from?" Elizabeth asked curiously.

"Kennebunkport, Maine. He's a terrific yachtsman, and he's a great dancer, too. Which brings me to the subject I know you've all been waiting for."

"Another party," Jessica said.

Lila frowned at her. "Not just *a* party, Jess. *The* party. *The* party of the year. I already talked to Daddy, and he said the sky's the limit. So we're throwing the biggest and best bash ever. We're going to get a really good band from L.A., maybe the Number One if they're not booked already. And I thought it would be fun to have it be a costume party, don't you think? I haven't had one in a long time."

Jessica's face lit up. "That's a great idea," she said enthusiastically.

15

Elizabeth and Enid exchanged glances. Apparently Jessica had a good idea for a costume!

"And," Lila said dramatically, "we're going to have really good food. Maybe even a lobster dinner!"

"I'll come as a lobster," Winston said, grinning at her. "That is, if I'm invited," he added hastily.

"When's the party going to be, Lila?" Elizabeth asked.

"Two weeks from this coming Saturday," Lila said. "I'll remind you," she added quickly. "Daddy's letting me print up invitations. You'll all get one."

"Amy will be here then," Elizabeth reminded her.

Lila frowned. "Don't worry, Liz. I'd be delighted to invite Amy Sutton. This is going to be such a big bash that there's plenty of room, even for tomboys."

Elizabeth bit her lip. She didn't like the way Lila sounded when she talked about Amy.

Elizabeth wanted her old friend to fit in at Sweet Valley High. Not that being friendly with Lila Fowler mattered to Elizabeth. She cared much more about getting Amy involved with *The Oracle*, introducing her to her closest friends, and making sure she felt welcome and happy.

She just hoped that Amy would find a warm reception when she finally moved back!

*　　*　　*

16

Enid Rollins loved walking home from school. For one thing, it was a chance to sort out what had taken place during the day. And the neighborhood was so pretty. She loved looking at the houses, the bright green lawns, the richly scented flowers. From certain places she could even see the nearby ocean, sparkling as the sunlight hit it.

But that afternoon Enid wasn't paying much attention to her surroundings. She was thinking about Elizabeth—and about Amy Sutton.

Enid had never met Amy. Unlike most of her classmates, she hadn't gone to elementary school in Sweet Valley. In fact, she hadn't moved there until she was in eighth grade, right after her parents split up.

She hadn't met Elizabeth right away, either. In fact, Enid had gone through a rough transition period after she moved in. Depressed about her parents' divorce, she had gotten mixed up with the wrong kids, the sort who were trouble in almost every way and were involved with drugs. Her boyfriend then was George Warren, who was older than Enid. They got into serious trouble together and eventually were separated when George was sent to boarding school. Enid was forced to face up to what she'd done. She went through a long withdrawn period, spending most of her time alone, usually buried in a book. Then, in tenth grade, she and Elizabeth became friends.

It was hard for Enid to sort out exactly what Elizabeth Wakefield meant to her. It wasn't just that Elizabeth had been a kind of model for Enid, then and afterward. Enid admired Elizabeth and counted on her advice and support. And that Elizabeth had helped her out of numerous scrapes. The one Enid could never forget was after the plane crash. . . .

Enid had stayed in touch with George, and when he came back to attend college in Sweet Valley, they put the pieces of their relationship back together. George had changed as much as Enid. He was sober, hard-working, earnest, and trying to realize a lifelong dream of becoming a pilot.

Enid and George were close for a long time. Enid had no idea that he had started to have strong feelings for Robin Wilson, whom he'd met in his flying class. George had planned on telling Enid after he had taken her for the plane ride he had promised her. However, after the two-seater plane crashed into Secca Lake, Enid was temporarily paralyzed, and George decided to postpone saying anything. An operation removed the pressure on Enid's spine, but to the doctor's surprise, she was still unable to walk. Only later did she realize a psychological block kept her from walking. It was Elizabeth who saved her . . . Elizabeth who had discovered what was going on between George and Robin and helped Enid to see that her fear of losing

George was preventing her from recovering completely.

But Enid's feelings about Elizabeth went far beyond gratitude. Enid often watched Elizabeth and Jessica with a mixture of amazement and envy. She couldn't imagine what it must be like to have a sister, let alone a twin, someone so like yourself in every way. Elizabeth was the closest thing Enid had to a sister. She realized now that she felt very possessive of her.

It was one thing sharing Elizabeth with Jessica. That was only natural. And for a long time, Elizabeth had gone out with Todd Wilkins, the brown-haired, handsome star of the basketball team. And Enid had had George. Elizabeth and Enid were used to weeks when they saw relatively little of each other. But since Enid and George had broken up and Todd had moved to Vermont, it seemed that she and Elizabeth were closer than ever. They often spent weekend evenings together, and Enid realized now that she had grown very dependent on her friend.

Maybe it'll do us good to spend less time together, she thought. But she didn't really believe it. Secretly she felt jealous of Amy Sutton. After all, Amy had known Elizabeth, Enid reflected, a lot longer than she had. And every time Elizabeth described her, Amy sounded more ideal. How could Enid possibly hope to compete with her?

Enid knew Elizabeth would never drop her for

Amy. That just wasn't the way Elizabeth operated. But all the same, she was anxious.

Elizabeth kept saying how much she wanted Enid and Amy to spend time together, to get to know each other. And Enid knew that, as always, Elizabeth's heart was in the right place. But she couldn't help wondering, with a sinking feeling in her stomach, what would happen if she didn't like Amy Sutton. Or if Amy Sutton didn't like her.

"Well, our very first column has gone off to the printer," Cara Walker said happily, swiveling around on the chair in the *Oracle* office to face Jessica. "What do you think? You think we're ready for national syndication? Or do we still need a little work?"

Jessica sighed. "The column's OK," she said moodily. Her mind wasn't on her role as half of Miss Lovelorn right then. The column was at the printer's, and the paper wouldn't come out until Wednesday. Jessica wasn't used to thinking about something so far out of sight. Besides, she had more pressing things on her mind.

Such as Jay McGuire.

It had been a long time since Jessica had fallen in love like this; painfully, breathtakingly, heartbreakingly in love. Every time she saw him her stomach did flip-flops. She had even started arranging to run into him between classes.

French, the one class they had together, was delicious torture. She spent the whole hour staring at him and by some sort of incredible fluke had managed to get him for her dialogue partner. This week they were pretending to be tour guides, learning the names of famous sites in Paris, but Jessica couldn't concentrate, she was so busy studying Jay.

He was gorgeous. About six feet tall, with sandy hair and the most fabulous green eyes with gold highlights in them. Jessica had always thought he was cute, but when their gazes locked after class one day, Jessica knew that true love between them was destined. *Jay McGuire.* Jessica loved saying his name to herself, and she had already figured out their future, step by step. She was certain he liked her, too. She had been turning the charm on full force every day in French, and if it weren't for one tiny little problem, Jessica was sure they'd be conversing outside class as well as in. If only she could get rid of that one little problem . . .

The problem was Denise Hadley.

Jay and Denise had been going out for a couple of months. And from the look of it, Jay was hooked—even Jessica had to admit that. Denise was a senior, a striking redhead with almond-shaped brown eyes and a knockout figure. Jessica didn't know her very well, but she would have liked her a lot more if she hadn't thrown herself at Jay. Jessica was convinced that was what had happened. Jay would probably drop Denise in a minute and realize Jessica was the one woman of his dreams if only she could think of *some* way . . .

"Jess." Cara pouted. "You're not listening to a single thing I'm saying. What's with you this afternoon?"

"Sorry," Jessica said, sighing miserably. "Cara, I think *I* need Miss Lovelorn's advice."

"Try me," Cara said, bright-eyed. "It can't be *that* bad," she added, seeing the look on Jessica's face.

"Try this, then," Jessica mumbled. " 'Dear Miss Lovelorn,' " she improvised, " 'I am madly, desperately in love with Jay McGuire. The only problem is Jay McGuire is madly in love with Denise Hadley. What should I do?' "

Cara stared at Jessica. "Jay McGuire . . . oh, dear. How long have he and Denise been going out?"

"Forever," Jessica moaned. "Anyway, for *months*. I think it really is desperate."

"Can't you fall in love with someone who isn't already taken?"

Jessica stared glumly at her.

"Hmmm," Cara said quickly. "I guess not. Well, in *that* case . . ."

"It's not even as though she's any good for him," Jessica pointed out. "I mean, she's over a year older than he is. She's old enough to be his—his—"

"Girlfriend," Cara cut in, and giggled.

Jessica glared at her. "Come on, Cara. She really is a lot older than he is. I mean, what's he going to do next year when she's in college? It's crazy. Besides, all her friends are seniors. He needs a junior. That's obvious. If only—"

Cara smiled at her. "Well, maybe working on the column will take your mind off him," she said, picking up some letters and tossing them onto the desk in front of Jessica. Jessica stared at the letters, her eyes widening as a wonderful idea began to take shape. "What about using the column to get a message to Jay McGuire?" she said craftily.

Cara stared at her. "You mean—"

"Run a letter or two from an older woman. Or a younger man. You know, something really clever. That's what I'm famous for, isn't it?"

Cara stared at Jessica, her eyes troubled. "Jessica, you're awful. Do you mean you're going to use the column to convince Jay that Denise is wrong for him?"

Jessica grinned. "Isn't it perfect? 'Cause once he's figured *that* out—"

"Once he's figured that out," Cara said wryly, "all I can say is, I hope the poor guy has insurance! Either that, or that he's Jessica-proof. Because if he isn't, he's got a rough couple of weeks ahead."

Jessica jumped up. "You know something?" she exclaimed, grabbing a piece of paper and slipping it into the typewriter. "I have a feeling I'm really going to do all right in the creative business after all!"

Cara laughed. "All I can say is, wherever you are, Denise Hadley, you'd better look out. Because with Jessica Wakefield and Miss Love-lorn *both* working against you, you probably won't have a chance!"

Three

"Where are you going?" Jessica mumbled from underneath her covers. It was ten o'clock on Saturday morning, but it might as well have been the middle of the night in Jessica's room, which the other Wakefields affectionately called "The Hershey Bar" because Jessica had painted it mud-brown one rainy afternoon.

Elizabeth had poked her head in the doorway to say goodbye. "I'm supposed to meet Enid at the beach in half an hour," she told her sister. "Mom's gone out, and I thought I'd better wake you up before I left."

Jessica groaned as she sat up in bed. "The beach?" she mumbled sleepily. "What time is it?"

"It's ten o'clock," Elizabeth said and laughed when Jessica groaned again and lay back down. Elizabeth had a feeling it would be hours before Jessica emerged in public.

"Come join us later," she called over her shoulder, grabbing her big striped towel and running downstairs. She was about to step outside when the telephone rang.

"Liz," an excited, feminine voice exclaimed. "It's me, Amy!"

Elizabeth listened for the familiar buzz of long distance. To her surprise, it sounded as though Amy were calling from nearby! "Amy! But where are you?" she asked, feeling confused. This was Saturday. The Suttons weren't supposed to move in until the following day!

"Right here in Sweet Valley," Amy sang out. "At the Bradleys' house—or should I say, *our* house, now. And I'm surrounded by *millions* of crates and boxes," she added. "Liz, you should *see* this place! Daddy says it looks like we've got enough stuff to fill *two* houses!"

Elizabeth felt like jumping up and down. "You mean you're here, really and truly *here?* I have to see you," she said impulsively. "Can I come over right away?"

Amy giggled. "You may not want to stay long, the way this place looks," she warned. "But, of course, come on over! I was hoping you'd come," she added. "You know, the old place sure looks different, Liz."

"I'll be right over," Elizabeth promised. She glanced quickly at her watch. It was ten-fifteen. She's have plenty of time to drop by and give Amy a welcome hug before heading to the beach.

A few minutes later Elizabeth was getting out

of the red Fiat Spider the twins shared. The scene before her was one of chaos. An enormous moving van was parked in the drive, and men were rushing back and forth with boxes and furniture. In the middle of all the chaos Dyan Sutton, looking stunning in a white linen suit, was standing perfectly still and shouting directions to the movers.

"Mrs. Sutton!" Elizabeth called, moving forward.

The next thing she knew, Mrs. Sutton was engulfing her in a warm, perfumed hug. "Good heavens, Liz," Mrs. Sutton said, stepping back and looking her up and down. "I'd never have known it was you in a million years if Amy hadn't said— Excuse me!" she called to one of the movers. "That goes in the living room."

She turned back to Elizabeth and shrugged helplessly. "Moving," she said simply, shaking her head. "Wait till you see Amy," Mrs. Sutton added. "You'd never know her. She's—"

But Mrs. Sutton never got to finish her sentence. The next instant a bloodcurdling shriek resounded from the top of the drive, and Amy Sutton came barreling toward her old friend, her arms outstretched.

"Amy!" Elizabeth cried.

The two girls threw their arms around each other. For several minutes they were laughing and hugging and talking and making no sense at all. But at last Elizabeth extricated herself from

Amy's exuberant embrace long enough to get a good look at her.

"Good lord, Amy," she said, shaking her head. "You never told me you got so beautiful!"

When Amy had left Sweet Valley after sixth grade, she was a skinny kid who needed braces. Now . . . well, Elizabeth could hardly believe her eyes. Amy was an inch or two taller than Elizabeth and slender, with dark-blond hair that fell to her shoulders. Her eyes, a slate-gray color, were outlined with gray pencil. Her smile was flawless. She looked, Elizabeth thought with admiration, like a fashion model. She was wearing a cotton miniskirt and a T-shirt, and even in that outfit she would have looked at home in any of the top fashion magazines.

"What about you, Liz? You're the one who's a knockout. Oh, Liz, it's so wonderful to actually *see* you again! And now that I'm back in Sweet Valley, it'll be just like old times."

"I feel like I have to pinch myself," Elizabeth whispered. "I just can't believe it's really happening. I didn't even expect you till tomorrow!"

"Well, we were all just in such a panic," Amy said, running her eyes speculatively over the chaos in the driveway. "You see, we were waiting until Mom knew about the contract and the station, and then we wanted to leave tomorrow but the moving company had scheduled to drop off all our stuff today. I was going to call you last night before we left, but I ran out of time. I was at this party— Oh, Lord, I have *so* much to tell you!"

Elizabeth hugged her. "We've got all the time in the world, now. You're practically my next-door neighbor!"

Amy frowned at the yellow dresser being carried past them. "That's mine. Recognize it?" she asked Elizabeth. "Goodness knows how I'll ever be able to sleep in that room tonight, though. It looks as if people have been dynamiting in there!"

Elizabeth grabbed Amy's arm. "Come over to my house," she said impulsively. "And spend the night tonight. Please, Amy, it'll be so much fun! And it'll give us a chance to start catching up."

Amy's face lit up. "What a great idea! If my parents don't mind," she added, sighing as she surveyed the driveway once more. "I'd hate to desert them now."

"Who's deserting whom?" Mr. Sutton demanded, coming over and giving Elizabeth a big kiss on the cheek. His blue eyes twinkled. "I hate to say it, but, boy, have you grown up since I last saw you!" he told her.

"Elizabeth wants me to go over to her house and spend the night," Amy said. "I don't suppose . . ."

"That's fine with me," her father told her, smiling at them both. "Who am I to wreck a great reunion? Just check with your mom, and get lost, you two!''

For the next half hour or so Elizabeth chatted with the Suttons, waiting for Amy to collect some clothing to take with her. She felt vaguely uneasy about something, but couldn't quite place what it was. Not until she and Amy were driving back to the Wakefields' house and the radio announcer said it was eleven-thirty did Elizabeth realize that she had forgotten about Enid.

''Omigod!'' she cried, slapping her forehead. ''I forgot Enid. I was supposed to meet her at the beach. It's so late she may have gone back home. I'll have to try to call her from the house.''

''Who's Enid?'' Amy asked, unwrapping a stick of gum and popping it into her mouth.

Elizabeth glanced at her. ''Oh, Amy, she's terrific! I know you're going to just adore each other. She's a special friend of mine. In fact, we were planning a ski trip together, and we put it off because Enid hoped that you could come, too. She's—''

''Ski trip?'' Amy smiled. ''Liz, I've got to tell you about this fabulous guy I met when I was skiing in Vermont. His name's John Norton. He's such a *doll*!''

''I'd love to hear about him,'' Elizabeth said, smiling at her. They were in front of the Wakefields' house now, and she parked the car in the drive. ''Jess is probably still in bed,'' she said to

Amy, "even though I woke her up at ten. Go on," she added. "What's John like?"

Amy pretended to swoon. "Incredible! Anyway, it turned into a really big thing. I mean, *really* big. In fact, he threatened to do something drastic when I left. He said he just couldn't *stand* the thought of our being separated. So I told him—"

"Look," Elizabeth cut in. "Jess is waving at you from the upstairs window."

Sure enough, there was Jessica, still in her nightgown, waving her arms like a madwoman.

"Come on in," Elizabeth said warmly to her friend. "I just want to call Enid's house and see if she went back there when I didn't show up."

She saw her father out on the patio and waved to him. A minute later Ned Wakefield came in to welcome Amy. Tall, dark, with brown hair and eyes, Mr. Wakefield looked like an older version of the twins' eighteen-year-old brother, Steven, who was away at college. He chatted with Amy for a while before returning to the patio, where he was soon immersed in reading the morning paper.

Elizabeth left Amy in the living room, then quickly went to the kitchen to call Enid. The phone rang twelve times before she replaced the receiver. Apparently no one was home. Did that mean Enid was still at the beach? Elizabeth felt terrible. She couldn't believe she'd been so thoughtless. She thought about getting in the car

31

and running over to the beach to see if Enid was still there, but it seemed unfair to Amy. *Enid will understand*, she told herself, not feeling entirely sure she was right but not certain what else to do about it, either.

When she walked into the living room, she saw that Jessica had come downstairs. She and Amy were talking a mile a minute. Elizabeth felt a strange twinge as she stood in the doorway and watched them, shoulder to shoulder on the couch, their faces animated. But she pushed the twinge aside and plopped down beside them. "OK, Amy Sutton," she said, laughing. "We'd better get started. We've got five years of catching up to do!"

It was almost midnight, and Amy and the twins were in Elizabeth's room, talking and giggling over the old yearbooks Jessica had dug out from grade school and junior high. "Liz, you look so weird!" she said laughing and pointing at a picture of her twin that had always cracked her up.

Elizabeth had had a wonderful day being with Amy again, and she had managed to push Enid to the back of her mind. To her surprise and delight, Amy and Jessica were actually getting along well. Jessica seemed absolutely fascinated by Amy's stories about Connecticut and John Norton. Apparently Dyan Sutton had started to do some traveling, and she had taken Amy with her, so the twins heard all about cricket in the Caribbean and golf in Florida. Most of Amy's stories involved romance in one way or another, and Elizabeth was beginning to feel that Amy Sutton was a little boy-crazy. But Elizabeth didn't really blame her. With her looks, Elizabeth thought, Amy must get so much attention!

"But Johnny really is a problem now," Amy confided to Jessica and Elizabeth. "I mean, at first I was flattered that he was going to miss me so much. But I certainly don't want anything long distance. It's the kiss of death when you move to a new place!"

Jessica seemed delighted. "I couldn't agree more," she said warmly, shooting Elizabeth a meaningful glance. Jessica had tried to convince Elizabeth of the same thing when Todd Wilkins moved away, though Elizabeth hadn't listened, and the relationship had continued for several months before she and Todd decided to break it off and just remain friends.

"The thing is," Amy added, leaning forward, "I want to meet some really wonderful guys right here in Sweet Valley. You two will have to help me," she added. "I won't know anyone at school, and I'm sure I'll be unbelievably shy at first, but still—"

Jessica giggled, "I think you'll be OK. What do you think, Liz?"

33

Elizabeth laughed. "I think you'll do just fine, Amy. You don't seem one bit shy to me!"

But she was listening to the conversation with only half an ear. All day she had been feeling uneasy about Enid, and try as she might, she just couldn't put her friend out of her mind.

She wasn't going to feel better until she knew Enid had forgiven her for standing her up that morning at the beach.

Four

"Hi, Mom," Elizabeth said, giving her mother an impulsive hug as she came up from behind her in the sun-filled kitchen. Alice Wakefield put down the Sunday paper, her blue eyes crinkling up at the corners as she smiled at her daughter. Slim, blond, and attractive, Mrs. Wakefield could still share clothing with her twin daughters and was sometimes mistaken for their older sister. Her youthful energy and sense of humor helped her keep up with Jessica and Elizabeth at all times.

"Where's Amy?" Mrs. Wakefield asked.

Elizabeth smiled. "Sound alseep. So's Jess, so I thought I'd sneak down here and see if I can't get hold of Enid before she disappears again today. Honestly," she added, looking perturbed as she recalled the events of the previous day, "I feel so guilty. Imagine poor Enid waiting for me at the beach. She must've been furious when I didn't show up!"

Mrs. Wakefield smiled gently. "You and Enid

35

have been through an awful lot together," she reminded her daughter. "I don't think an accidental slip-up or two will be the end of your friendship!"

"I hope you're right," Elizabeth said. A minute later she was heading out of the kitchen. "Anyway," she called back over her shoulder, "I've just come up with a wonderful idea."

"What's that?" her mother asked, picking up the home design section and opening it.

"Brunch," Elizabeth said with obvious satisfaction. "A good old-fashioned brunch at the Pancake House—that's what. Don't you think that's a perfect way to introduce Amy and Enid?"

But she didn't wait for her mother's reply. She raced to the den, picked up the receiver of the phone, and began dialing Enid's number, humming to herself as she imagined the wonderful time the three of them would have together.

Enid and Amy would meet each other at last! Elizabeth thought. She couldn't wait. She was convinced that once Enid met Amy Sutton, she would forgive her for everything. And the sooner the two girls met, the better!

"So you see, Enid," Elizabeth said rapidly, "in all the excitement, I completely forgot the time. And when I realized what had happened, it was already eleven-thirty! I tried calling," she added apologetically, "but no one was home."

Enid didn't say anything at first. "Oh," she said finally, her voice curiously flat.

"Enid!" Elizabeth cried, anguished. "I feel like a rat about the whole thing. In fact, I couldn't stop thinking about it all day," she said honestly. "You have to tell me you forgive me. Otherwise, I'll—I'll—"

Enid laughed at the desperate sound in her friend's voice. "OK, OK," she said, relenting. "I admit it. I was livid. But I can see now how it happened."

"Enid, you're fantastic," Elizabeth said, a wave of relief flooding over her. She felt a million times better the second Enid laughed. It was the first sign that everything was going to be all right between them again. "It won't happen again, Enid," she promised warmly. "Now that Amy's moved in—"

"That's the thing, Liz," Enid said in a small voice. "I know this sounds really stupid, but I can't help feeling that her being here is going to change everything. You know the old saying: 'Two's company. Three's a crowd.' Well, I feel sort of like the third member of the party, if you see what I mean."

"That's crazy," Elizabeth said passionately. "Enid, what are you saying? Don't you realize that you're my very best friend in the whole world?"

Enid didn't answer, and Elizabeth bit her lip. "Look," she said, twisting the telephone cord into a knot, "why don't the three of us get together so you can see for yourself how fabulous Amy is? How about brunch later on this morning at the Pancake House?"

"If you want to," Enid said doubtfully. "But don't you think—"

"I think it's high time you and Amy met each other," Elizabeth said firmly. "You're going to love each other! Trust me, Enid," she added, a note of determination in her voice.

An hour later Elizabeth and Amy were on their way to the restaurant to meet Enid. Elizabeth couldn't believe her eyes when she saw the outfit Amy had packed in her overnight case. She looked so *glamorous* in a black jumpsuit and boots, which even Jessica had to admit were ahead of fashion.

"We're only going to the Pancake House," Elizabeth had warned Amy, feeling ordinary in a cotton sweater and a pair of corduroy jeans.

Amy had looked dismissively at her reflection. "You can never tell," she told Elizabeth conspiratorially. "We might meet a handsome stranger on the way." Her gray eyes widened. "We might even meet a movie star!"

Elizabeth laughed. "More likely we'll just meet a waiter," she said dryly.

Now, glancing occasionally into the rearview mirror at the traffic behind her, Elizabeth told

Amy all about Enid. Or at least, she *tried* to tell Amy all about Enid. It seemed kind of hard to get a word in edgewise once Amy got her teeth into her favorite subject.

"I had a dream last night about John Norton," she confided, rolling down her window and taking a pair of black sunglasses out of her purse. "It was incredible! Liz, do you suppose I miss him more than I think I do?"

Elizabeth laughed. "Sounds kind of like you do," she admitted. "Now, Amy—about Enid. I just want to fill you in on some of the background stuff so you two can—"

"Liz," Amy said, dimpling as she smiled warmly at Elizabeth, "don't worry about a thing. Enid and I will get along just fine!"

Elizabeth looked sheepish. She hadn't realized that her motives were so transparent. "You know how it is," she mumbled awkwardly. "I care so much about you both, and I just want you two to like each other as much as I like both of you!"

"You're such a doll," Amy said fondly. "How in the world could I *not* adore a friend of yours?"

Elizabeth was about to answer when Amy leaned forward, an expression of amazed delight on her face. "Look!" she gasped, pointing out the window at a blond boy on a bicycle. "Isn't he gorgeous, Liz? Gosh," she said, settling back in her seat, "I have a feeling being back in California is going to be even more fun than I expected!"

Elizabeth smiled as she pulled the Fiat into the parking lot in front of the Pancake House. Mrs. Rollins's light blue car was parked in the lot. Enid was already there.

Suddenly Elizabeth's anxiety melted away. She was sure the brunch would go beautifully. "Amy," she said, putting her arm around her friend as they walked into the restaurant, "I have a feeling you're right. And with you around, living in Sweet Valley is going to be more fun than ever before!"

"Hmmm," Amy said, looking critically at the menu. "I think I'll have a grapefruit," she told the waitress. "And black coffee, please."

Elizabeth and Enid exchanged glances. "Grapefruit?" Elizabeth repeated, staring at Amy. "That isn't *all* you're having, is it?"

Amy smiled. "I have to be careful," she told them. "I really *hate* myself if I weigh a single ounce over one-hundred and ten pounds."

Enid gulped. Her own order—blueberry pancakes, orange juice, and tea—seemed huge in comparison.

"I'll have pancakes, too," Elizabeth said, smiling at Enid.

"*You* never had to worry, Liz," Amy said

reflectively, toying with her spoon. "Some people have all the luck!"

Enid didn't say anything. Eyes downcast, she was fiddling with her silverware, too.

"Remember how much we used to eat after school?" Amy said, giggling. "Enough to choke a horse! Twinkies, milkshakes, those peanut-butter cookies your mother made."

"But your mother bought the best food," Elizabeth reminded her. She turned to Enid, trying to bring her into the conversation. "You should've seen the Suttons' cupboards! It was like having a candy store in the kitchen. We used to eat until we felt sick." She burst out laughing, remembering.

"Sounds like you two had a lot of fun," Enid said flatly.

Amy raised her eyebrows. "Fun?" She burst into giggles. "The two of us got into so many scrapes! Remember the time we locked our bicycles together and couldn't get them undone?"

Elizabeth groaned, remembering. "We had to drag them all the way home. We must've looked so silly."

"And the time we tried on my mother's clothes and she caught us?"

"Sounds great," Enid said, still fiddling with her silverware. "Sounds like you two—"

"Look!" Amy interrupted, smiling. "The food's here."

"Have some of my pancakes," Elizabeth begged Amy, pushing her plate toward her.

Amy shook her head. "No, thanks," she said vehemently, looking out of the corner of her eye as Enid took a pat of butter to float in her golden syrup.

Enid took a deep breath. Elizabeth smiled at her, thinking, *This isn't so bad! I wonder what I was worried about.*

"How does it feel being back in Sweet Valley?" Enid asked. It was the first real question she'd been able to ask Amy. And she did want to make an effort.

Amy picked at the edge of her grapefruit. "It's great," she said warmly. "Of course, I'm a little worried about fitting in at school and everything. Back at home . . . well, I guess moving is always a scary thing, whatever age you are."

Enid blinked. Somehow it was hard to believe this poised, glamorous girl could be worried about anything. "You're not worried about the schoolwork," she said tentatively, taking a bite of pancakes.

"Schoolwork?" Amy stared at her, her gray eyes round with incredulity. "Who cares about schoolwork?" She tossed her hair back and gave Enid a charming smile. "No," she confided, "I guess I'm just a little shy, that's all."

Shy, Enid thought skeptically. *Who is she trying to kid?*

She looked across the table at Elizabeth, certain her friend would look disapproving or at least surprised. Enid had always valued Elizabeth's taste and judgment. She must realize that Amy Sutton was acting like a total airhead!

But to her shock, Elizabeth was smiling fondly at Amy across the table. "You'll fit in just fine," she said enthusiastically. "Won't she, Enid?"

Enid gulped. "Uh—yes," she said quickly. "Of course she will."

"Maybe we can meet after school tomorrow, and I can take you around the *Oracle* office," Elizabeth said to Amy. "I know you'll love it! It's a lot better organized than the sixth grade paper you and I put together, Amy."

"*The Oracle?*" Amy repeated blankly. "Oh, is that the school paper? The one Jess is doing the 'Miss Lovelorn' column for?"

"*Elizabeth* writes the 'Eyes and Ears' column," Enid pointed out loyally. "She's one of the most important members of the *Oracle* staff."

Amy lifted her eyebrows. "Really? Liz, that's terrific. I'd be absolutely thrilled if you'd sort of show me the ropes, just for the first few days. And you too, Enid," she added, turning to the brown-haired girl and smiling again. The smile struck Enid as one-hundred-percent insincere.

Enid bit her lip. She didn't know what to say.

"Would you two just excuse me for a second?" Amy asked, bouncing up from the table and heading for the ladies' room before either of them could answer.

Smiling, Elizabeth leaned forward. "Isn't she terrific, Enid? I told you she's really easy to talk to!"

Enid put her fork down. Suddenly her appetite seemed to have left her. She looked long and hard at Elizabeth's expression. Elizabeth was being serious, she decided. She really liked this girl. But after all, Amy Sutton had been her best friend. Of course she thought Amy was terrific!

Enid looked away uneasily. She could hardly tell Elizabeth the truth: that she thought Amy Sutton was vain and silly. That wasn't exactly the way to ease an awkward situation.

"She seems very nice," she lied, taking a deep breath and waiting for Elizabeth, who knew Enid better than anyone else, to look up and ask what was wrong.

But Elizabeth didn't seem to realize that Enid was upset. "I'm so glad you think so," Elizabeth said emphatically. "If you two hadn't liked each other, I just don't know *what* I would have done."

Enid gulped, staring at Elizabeth without saying a word. Elizabeth, Enid thought, was being oblivious to her feelings. And to Amy Sutton's feelings, too. Because Enid was pretty sure that Amy had liked *her* even less than she had liked Amy!

Poor Elizabeth, Enid thought compassionately, staring across the table at her friend. She was so sweet and good-natured that she didn't realize that her two friends hadn't exactly hit it off.

One thing was certain. Enid wasn't going to be the one to let her friend in on the awful truth!

Five

"Well, Liz," Lila Fowler crooned, plopping down beside Elizabeth on the plush lawn in front of Sweet Valley High, "it looks like your concern for your friend was pretty unfounded. I've never seen a girl get such a warm welcome!"

Shading her eyes with her hand, Elizabeth smiled. Amy was standing on the patio outside the cafeteria, surrounded by a crowd of admirers. Lila was right, Elizabeth told herself. She would never have guessed Amy's first few days of school would be like this!

It was Wednesday at lunchtime, and already Amy seemed to have a million friends. Every time Elizabeth saw her she was surrounded—even while walking from class to class. It looked as though Amy Sutton was an undeniable hit.

Elizabeth couldn't have been happier for her friend. She glowed when people praised Amy in front of her, and she'd done her best to make sure every one of her friends knew just how terrific Amy Sutton was.

Only one thing made Elizabeth feel a twinge of uneasiness. And that was the surprising camaraderie between Amy and her sister, Jessica.

It wasn't that Elizabeth didn't want the two of them to get along. Her first reaction to their newfound friendship was immense relief. Jessica had been aloof toward Amy before she moved away, and Elizabeth had been convinced that the two of them would never hit it off when Amy returned. Jessica never liked Elizabeth's friends.

When it became apparent that Amy and Jessica were more than willing to take a new look at each other, Elizabeth was delighted. It made having Amy around even more fun. But, well, Elizabeth had to admit she'd been feeling a few twinges of jealousy lately. It seemed to her that Jessica had completely taken over her friend! *Jessica* was the one who was really showing Amy around. Jessica was introducing Amy to *her* friends, giving her a tour of the school, and—this was the part Elizabeth hated to admit, even to herself. She adored her twin sister and would never allow herself a disloyal thought, but she didn't want Jessica wasting Amy's time with trivial things such as the sorority or cheerleading or endless gossip about boys. Elizabeth knew Amy too well for that. The poor girl would be bored stiff in a matter of days!

"Amy's fabulous," Lila went on, her brown eyes intent on Elizabeth's. "Why didn't you tell me she'd turned into such a knockout?" she added accusingly.

Elizabeth picked a blade of grass. "Well, I hadn't seen her in years. Anyway, I don't think it's her most important quality," she said, trying to keep her voice light.

Lila shrugged. "Well, she certainly seems to be doing all right around here," she said. There was an annoyed tinge to her voice, "Kind of silly for you to have worried about her fitting in, don't you think?" With that she strolled off, still frowning.

"What's bothering her?" Enid demanded. She had approached just in time to hear Lila's last remark, and her green eyes were bright with curiosity.

"Oh, nothing," Elizabeth said, trying to laugh. For some reason she didn't feel like burdening Enid with another Amy Sutton story. "You know how Lila is," she added vaguely.

Enid smiled. "I sure do." As she sank down on the grass, she had a thoughtful expression on her face. "Liz, I didn't want to bring this up earlier, but I really have to let my aunt know what our plans are. I talked to her last night, and she said the best time for her would be next weekend. How does that sound to you?"

Elizabeth thought for a minute. "Sounds great," she said, grinning at her friend. "All systems go!"

Enid bit her lip. "The only possible catch is

48

Lila's party for her cousin Christopher. That's next Saturday night, isn't it?"

Elizabeth's face clouded over briefly. "Oh, who cares about another one of Lila Fowler's parties!" she said. "I'd rather go up to Lake Tahoe any day."

"Good," Enid said happily. "I was hoping you'd say that. I mean just between the two of us, I can't imagine this party's going to be that much different from any of her other big bashes."

Elizabeth smiled. "Though it *would* be kind of fun to meet Christopher. Lila says he may drop by school one day, but he hasn't so far."

Enid shrugged. "If you can pass up the party, I sure can. But, Liz"—she toyed with the hem of her skirt—"do you still want me to invite Amy?"

Elizabeth looked closely at her friend. "Do you still want her to come?" she asked seriously.

Enid's face reddened. She didn't want Elizabeth to know what a bad impression Amy Sutton had made on her so far. Since Elizabeth seemed to like Amy so much, Enid didn't want to influence her opinion. "I'd like her to come," she mumbled. "But I just thought *you* might want to ask her, since you know her so much better than I do."

"You've got it," she said playfully. "I'll ask her the very first chance I get."

Her aqua eyes narrowed thoughtfully as she watched Amy across the lawn, giggling and talking animatedly with Jessica, Cara Walker, and a crowd of their sorority friends. It would be good to get Amy and Enid alone together for a weekend, she told herself firmly. Once the three of them got away from school—away from Sweet Valley . . .

Elizabeth had to admit that it didn't look as if Enid and Amy had been that crazy about each other at the Pancake House on Sunday morning. But she was sure that that had been due to the circumstances. Once they really got to know each other, she was absolutely sure the two of them would get along perfectly!

Still, for the first time, listening to Amy's piercing giggle, Elizabeth felt a pang of uneasiness. What if her two best friends didn't get along? she asked herself. What in the world was she going to do then?

A big group inside the cafeteria had gathered around Olivia Davidson, a pert, slender junior who was the arts editor for *The Oracle*. Olivia was reading aloud from the "Miss Lovelorn" column in the latest edition of *The Oracle*, which had come out that day. This was the second week the column had run, and it was already a big hit.

"Come on, Liv," Winston Egbert begged. "Tell us what our sage love counselors have to tell us today."

Olivia giggled. "OK, here's the first letter. 'Dear Miss Lovelorn,' " she read aloud, " 'I have this problem. I'm a junior, and my girlfriend is a senior. The thing is, the gap didn't bother me at first, but now it's really starting to get to me. She doesn't know any of my friends and always insists we spend time with hers. Even worse, because she's a year older, she acts so bossy about certain things! Should I be looking around for someone younger, or do you think the age difference doesn't matter?' "

Winston let out a long, low whistle. "What does Miss Lovelorn have to say to *that*?"

Olivia's eyes quickly scanned the page. "It's signed 'Cradle-Snatched.' She writes back: 'Dear Snatched. Wise up! She is obviously in another world. Why don't you give a girl your own age a chance?' "

"Pretty harsh," Roger Patman, Olivia's boyfriend, remarked. "Are there any more letters?"

Olivia nodded. "Miss Lovelorn obviously chose this as the theme of the day. Listen to the second one: 'Dear Miss Lovelorn: I'm a senior, and my boyfriend's a year younger than me. The problem is my friends tease me all the time. They ask me what I'm going to do next year when I go away to college, and the truth is, I'm getting sick and tired of the whole thing. At first I thought love could overcome anything, but I'm beginning to lose faith. Sometimes I think I need a man, not a boy. What advice can you give me?' Signed, 'Older, Not Wiser.' "

Winston moaned and pretended to clutch his

heart. "This is sadder than Romeo and Juliet," he cried.

"Cut it out, Winston," Lila Fowler said, leaning forward attentively. "Go on, Olivia. What does Miss Lovelorn say?"

" 'Dear Older,' " Olivia read aloud. " 'Time to wise up. Listen to your friends and Miss Lovelorn: face the truth before it's too late. He's wrong for you. Let him know it before you *really* hurt him.' "

Lila snuck a look at the paper over Olivia's shoulder. "Can True Love Last Despite Age Difference?" the headline ran. "Kind of coincidental," she mused, catching Olivia's eye. "Are you thinking what I'm thinking?"

"Jay McGuire and Denise Hadley," Olivia said, putting her paper down. "Sure sounds like them, doesn't it?"

"You think Jay and Denise each wrote to Miss Lovelorn without the other one knowing—and that Cara and Jessica printed the letters even so?" Winston demanded.

"Boy, are they in for a surprise if that's the case!" Lila giggled. "Look!" she cried a minute later, spotting Jessica and Amy across the crowded cafeteria. "There's Jess now. I don't know about you guys, but I intend to ask Miss Lovelorn herself!"

Jessica lifted her eyebrows, her aquamarine

eyes wide with innocence. "Lila Fowler," she crooned sweetly, "all I can tell you is that our job as editors is to print what we get. Can I help it if two letters on the same theme came in last week?"

Lila stared at her. "You never tell me anything anymore," she grumbled. "Since Amy Sutton moved here, you're acting like a stranger."

Jessica smiled winningly at Lila. "And what about you? Your handsome cousin's been in town for three whole days, and you haven't even invited me over to meet him."

Lila frowned. "That's because he went to L.A. on Sunday morning, and he's not coming back till next weekend. He's leaving *me* all the work for the party," she added, pouting.

"It's still going to be a costume party, isn't it?" Jessica demanded, her face brightening.

Lila nodded. "Who're you going to come as, Jess?"

"It wouldn't be any fun if I gave it away now, would it?" Jessica cooed.

She barely noticed the sulky expression on Lila's face. Jessica was too intent on a scene taking place at the back of the cafeteria. Jay McGuire was sitting at a table, his head in his hands. Denise Hadley was beside him. And neither of them looked one bit happy.

Jessica knew the most she could hope for was that the letters she had printed in that week's paper would make them take a long look at how futile their relationship was. She knew neither would ever really believe the other had written the letters. All she wanted was to get them thinking—and arguing.

Jessica was more than ready to do the rest, once Jay gave her the signal. And from the glum look on his face right then, she had a feeling she wouldn't have long to wait.

"Amy!" Elizabeth called, out of breath. The blonde didn't turn around, and Elizabeth quickened her speed as she hurried through the crowded hall. The last bell had just rung, and she wanted to get hold of Amy before she disappeared. Elizabeth still hadn't gotten a chance to show her friend the *Oracle* office.

"Liz!" Amy exclaimed, spinning around and smiling when Elizabeth grabbed her arm. "What is it?" she demanded. "You've been running. Is something the matter?"

"No," Elizabeth said, pausing to catch her breath and laughing. "It's just that you're so hard to get hold of! I thought we were going to have lunch together today," she added.

Amy's gray eyes filled with horror. "Lunch!" She clapped her hand to her forehead. "Liz, I don't know what's wrong with me," she said as they walked down the hall together. "I've been *so* busy. I never realized meeting new people took so much time!"

Elizabeth smiled. It was impossible to get angry with Amy. All day she'd been feeling . . . well, almost out of sorts about her old friend. And now, all it took was that winning smile, and she felt ready to forgive Amy Sutton anything in the world.

"The reason I wanted to find you," Elizabeth said, "is that Enid asked me at lunch today about the ski trip we've been planning. Remember?"

Amy nodded. "Of course I remember. What's up?"

"Enid thinks that next weekend is the best time for her Aunt Nancy. But she wanted me to check with you before confirming the plans."

"Next weekend?" Amy asked. She shrugged. "Sounds fine to me."

Elizabeth stared at her. She'd expected Amy to be a little bit more excited. Enid was being char- acteristically warm and generous, offering to invite a virtual stranger to her aunt's cabin. And Amy seemed so nonchalant about it all.

"It sounds like fun," Amy said, giving Elizabeth an impulsive hug. "Honestly, Liz. Don't look so glum. We'll have a terrific time."

Elizabeth felt vastly relieved. "I know we will," she said happily. "Enid's been going to so much trouble, Amy. She's really made lots of plans with her aunt. I just know it's going to be great."

"Oh, look!" Amy exclaimed, her eyes lighting up. "There's Jessica and Cara. You don't mind if

I run off with them, do you? They promised to take me to cheerleading practice this afternoon."

Elizabeth stared at her. "Cheerleading practice? But I thought—"

"I adore cheerleading," Amy told her, her eyes shining. "I was on the squad at my old high school. Didn't you know?"

Elizabeth shook her head. "I wanted to show you the *Oracle* office," she said miserably. "Couldn't we just—"

"Some other time," Amy promised, hurrying down the hall toward Cara and Jessica.

Elizabeth bit her lip. She knew she wasn't being fair. Amy was new in town and needed to spend as much time as possible meeting people, getting used to Sweet Valley High, joining whatever activities she enjoyed. If she wanted to be a cheerleader . . .

But Elizabeth couldn't help feeling disappointed. It wasn't just that Amy seemed to prefer the things Jessica liked: boys, gossip, cheerleading. The real problem was that Amy didn't seem to have very much time for Elizabeth.

I must be doing something wrong, Elizabeth told herself. And she vowed then and there to improve her attitude, to be kinder and more generous with her friend. She was convinced if things were less than she'd expected, it must be her own fault. And she was willing to do practically anything to show Amy how deep her friendship ran.

Six

The twins were sitting at the big kitchen table in the Wakefields' sun-filled kitchen, dawdling over their raisin toast and cream cheese and reading the morning paper. Mr. Wakefield, whose law office was in Sweet Valley, had already left for work, and Mrs. Wakefield was upstairs putting the finishing touches on her makeup before going off to her interior design firm. Elizabeth looked at her watch and frowned. They had exactly ten minutes before they had to leave for school.

"I hate Monday mornings," Jessica groaned, throwing down the section of the paper she had been reading and stretching. "Especially after a weekend like this past one!"

Elizabeth regarded her twin. "What was so special about this weekend? If you ask me, it was just kind of average."

Jessica smiled mysteriously. "Oh, I don't know," she said, flipping her sun-streaked hair off her shoulders. "I guess when you're in love, *everything* feels special."

Elizabeth's eyebrows shot up. "In love?"

"Honestly, Liz. You make it sound like a disease. As a matter of fact, I happen to be sublimely happy."

"I see," Elizabeth remarked dryly. "Can I just ask who the lucky man is this time?" She giggled. "Or should I say, the lucky *victim*?"

Jessica's eyes filled with mock indignation. "My own sister," she moaned. "If you must know, the lucky man is none other than my dialogue partner—Jay McGuire."

Elizabeth stared at her sister. "Jay? But he's taken," she objected. Suddenly an expression of horror crossed her face. "Jessica," she said threateningly, "I don't suppose those letters in your column last week had anything to do with this latest crush of yours, did they?"

Jessica popped the last bite of toast into her mouth. "Liz," she said reprovingly, "how could you possibly suspect me of something so altogether low and conniving? Don't you think I have *any* respect for the honorable world of journalism?"

Elizabeth glared at her. "I'm not kidding, Jess," she fumed. "If you've been using *The Oracle* in one of your crazy schemes to get between two perfectly happy people—"

"That's where you're wrong, Liz," Jessica said sweetly. "Denise and Jay are *not* completely happy together. Even a total stranger could see that."

Elizabeth groaned. "Spare me," she said. "I don't know if I can stand this today. Just tell me one thing," she added, getting up and reaching for her books on the kitchen counter. "Have you and Jay actually been spending time together, or is this romance still in its planning stages?"

"Well," Jessica said, turquoise eyes lowered, "I *did* see him yesterday afternoon. I had to drop by his house to go over this tourist project we're doing for French."

Elizabeth shook her head. "Honestly, Jess, as long as I live, I doubt I'll ever fully come to grips with your awesome powers of persuasion!"

Jessica grinned modestly. "We'll see," she said lightly, grabbing her books and following Elizabeth to the door. They both called goodbye to their mother. Then Jessica went on, "The thing is, I've got to convince Jay to come with me to Lila's party. Don't you think he's adorable?"

Elizabeth smiled. "He's cute," she agreed. "Though from the impression I've gotten, Denise thinks so, too."

Jessica chose to ignore this. "Speaking of Lila's party," she said, "do you realize you haven't mentioned it one single time? Not even on Saturday when we got those fabulous invitations?"

Elizabeth laughed. "That's because I'm not going," she told her sister, getting into the driver's seat of the red Fiat Spider. "Which reminds

59

me—I really should let Lila know. She didn't ask for replies, but it still seems rude not to say anything."

Jessica was thunderstruck. "*Why?*" she shrieked. "Liz, this is going to be the best party to hit Sweet Valley in *months!*"

Elizabeth smiled at her. "I'm sure it'll be fun," she said lightly, "but this weekend Enid, Amy, and I are going skiing up near Lake Tahoe."

Jessica stared at her. "Skiing? With *Enid?*" She grimaced. "You'd trade that for an all-out bash at the Fowlers'? Didn't you hear that Lila's dad got the Number One to play?"

Elizabeth shrugged. "I'd rather go on the ski trip," she said firmly.

Jessica stared out the window. "And *Amy's* really going with you two?" she added skeptically.

"Yes," Elizabeth said, frowning. "Why shouldn't she?"

Jessica didn't answer for a minute. "You know, cheerleader auditions are this afternoon," she said casually, fiddling with the bright cotton scarf around her neck.

Elizabeth glanced at her. "Really?" She didn't understand the connection, and frankly, she wasn't that interested in what the cheerleaders did. "Who's trying out?" she asked.

Jessica held up one hand to tick off the names. She listed four or five. "And about eight or nine more," she said. She paused dramatically. "And Amy Sutton," she concluded.

Elizabeth tightened her grip on the wheel. "*Amy's* trying out for the cheerleading squad?"

Jessica studied her twin carefully. "Why shouldn't she?" she demanded. "I have a feeling she's really good. She was a cheerleader at her old school. And remember what a great baton twirler she was in sixth grade? She certainly has the spirit and the confidence. I have a feeling she's going to make it!"

Elizabeth bit her lip. Jessica was right, she reminded herself. Amy had every right in the world to try out for cheerleading, and it was none of Elizabeth's business. But secretly she couldn't help feeling disappointed. If Amy made the squad, Elizabeth would know she would probably see even less of her than she had so far. As it was, Elizabeth felt as though she had barely seen her friend. That past weekend, for example, Elizabeth had counted on getting together with Amy, taking her shopping or going to the beach with her. But Amy seemed to be busy all weekend long!

Also, unreasonable as it seemed, Elizabeth had counted on the fact that she and her old friend would still have dozens of things in common. The old Amy Sutton was someone Elizabeth could share anything with. They used to spend hours together talking about the future. Elizabeth had poured her heart out about her longing to be a writer, and Amy had listened attentively. Amy hadn't been sure what she wanted to be. But she was really good at sports and never cared what people thought about her or how she looked. She didn't like to dance—she had fallen down in the ballet class she and the twins had taken together! And now she wanted to be a cheerleader?

Elizabeth couldn't help feeling disappointed that her friend had changed so completely. "Well," Elizabeth said philosophically, pulling the Fiat into the parking lot at Sweet Valley High, "if Amy really does want to make the squad, I hope she does." She was quiet for a minute, her pretty face thoughtful. "In fact," she said, smiling at Jessica, "I just might come along this afternoon to watch the tryouts."

Amy Sutton might have changed a little, but she was still one of Elizabeth's best friends. And Elizabeth was determined to give her friend all the support she could.

Enid's brow wrinkled in surprise. "We have the whole afternoon off from school and you're going to watch the cheerleading auditions?" Clearly Enid hadn't expected her best friend to be interested enough to go along and watch.

"Amy's trying out," Elizabeth told her. "And I thought I'd just show up to give her a bit of support."

Enid bit her lip. In her opinion the last thing Amy Sutton needed was Elizabeth's support. But she didn't dare tell Elizabeth how she felt about Amy. Elizabeth would think she was jealous or that she just hadn't given the new girl a chance.

It had been over a week now, and Enid had watched Amy Sutton enough to be convinced the blond girl wasn't her type at all. In fact, everything she'd seen of Amy had strengthened her conviction that the girl was spoiled, selfish, and vain. She didn't like the way Amy treated Elizabeth, either. Enid had the distinct impression Amy was using Elizabeth, that she had time for her old friend only when she needed something.

It upset Enid to see Elizabeth being put through this. Elizabeth was so loyal, so trusting. Enid knew she would stick by Amy until Amy hurt her, something Enid was convinced was going to happen before long. But she knew she couldn't say any of this to Elizabeth without risking their friendship. Part of being a good friend to Elizabeth meant sitting by in silence now, however much it hurt.

"I know we were supposed to go shopping this afternoon," Elizabeth was saying, her aqua eyes troubled. "That's the only thing that's bothering me. We were going to the mall to look for ski gloves for this weekend!"

Enid's green eyes twinkled, "That was hardly

a date carved in stone," she teased Elizabeth. "We can just as easily go tomorrow. Don't give it a second thought."

Elizabeth frowned. She was grateful to Enid for being understanding, but she knew it was wrong to break the date. "No," she said firmly. "Let's just meet later. How about if I meet you in front of the Ski Shop at four o'clock?"

"Fine," Enid said. "Liz," she added impulsively, "I can't tell you how much I'm looking forward to this weekend!"

Elizabeth's face broke into a big smile. "Oh, Enid," she said happily, "I feel the same way." She looked intently at her friend. "Look," she added, putting her hand on Enid's arm, "I know you really haven't gotten a chance to get to know Amy yet. But this weekend—you'll see, Enid! You're going to like her just as much as I do!"

Enid forced a smile. "I'm sure I will, Liz," she said gently.

Enid's green eyes were thoughtful as she watched Elizabeth bound off for the football field, where the cheerleaders were holding auditions. Maybe Elizabeth was right, Enid thought hopefully. Maybe all Amy Sutton needed was another chance.

In any case, she assured herself, this weekend would reveal the truth once and for all. Enid just hoped for Elizabeth's sake that she was right, that Amy would turn out to be an absolute angel.

But she had a feeling that wasn't the way things were going to turn out at all.

"OK, everyone!" Robin Wilson, the pretty co-captain of the cheerleading squad called out to the group of girls waiting to audition. "You all know the routine. We're going to ask you to do it three times, and we'll each give you a score between one and ten points. At the end we'll add up the points and take a vote." Behind her, Ricky Capaldo, the manager of the squad, was collecting forms with each contestant's name, grade, and cheering experience.

Elizabeth was sitting on the sun-drenched bleachers with the cluster of classmates who had turned out to watch. There had been only morning classes that day due to an afternoon teachers' conference. Jessica and Robin were running the auditions, and Jessica, clipboard in hand, looked especially official. The other cheerleaders—Annie Whitman, Jean West, Cara Walker, Sandra Bacon, and Maria Santelli—were standing around attentively, waiting for the first girl to go through her routine.

Amy Sutton was the last girl to perform the simple cheering routine. The minute she had finished, Elizabeth knew she had made the team. Jessica was right. Amy was a natural. Years of sports had kept her in perfect condition, but now she moved with new grace. More important, she looked as if she were having fun, which none of the others had managed. She smiled each time she performed the routine, and her voice was perfect during the cheers—loud, but sweet at the same time.

At the end of the third round of auditions, Ricky Capaldo rounded up the cheerleaders to collect the scores, but Elizabeth felt confident it was a foregone conclusion for everyone involved. No one looked at all surprised when Amy Sutton was declared the newest member of the Sweet Valley High cheerleading squad.

"Phew," Jean West said, standing back a little from the crowd that had gathered around Amy. "I'm glad that's over. I was really dreading this afternoon. After the last time . . ."

Sandra Bacon nodded. She had been thinking about those auditions, too. Trying out for the squad had been a nightmare for Sandra. She and Jean were best friends, and Jean had been on the squad since her sophomore year. Naturally, Sandra wanted to try out, too, but she had made a fool of herself during the final auditions, when she fell down doing one of the jumps. She was never really sure how she'd gotten on the squad after making such a terrible mistake.

"She's really good, isn't she?" Jean asked, indicating Amy.

Sandra nodded. "She *is* good," she agreed.

"Hey!" Ricky Capaldo said, coming over to join them. "My two favorite cheerleaders," he joked. He hugged them both. "I was just telling Amy that the good thing about you two is that if you're looking for one, you always find the other. You're a real team!"

"You and your jokes," Jean scoffed, giggling.

Sandra didn't laugh, though. She was thinking that Ricky had probably said it differently to Amy. She could hear him saying, "Jeannie West and her little shadow. Everything Jeannie does, Sandra tries to do, too—only she never does it quite as well."

Jean often made Sandra feel inferior. She knew she wasn't as pretty as Jean, or as good in school. She couldn't do anything Jean couldn't do! As Ricky moved away, Sandra tried to smile, but the muscles in her face didn't seem to be behaving.

Jean didn't notice the serious expression on Sandra's face; she was too involved thinking about something. "Jess mentioned this afternoon that Pi Beta Alpha is starting a pledge season soon," Jean said slowly, tracing a triangle in the dust with her sneaker.

"That's right," Sandra said. Suddenly she felt embarrassed. "They must've decided at the last meeting," she said hastily. "I missed it, remember?"

Jean's cheeks reddened. "I don't suppose—"

Sandra felt a strange, uneasy sensation in her stomach. She knew what Jean was going to say.

Jean wasn't a member of the exclusive sorority, and she really wanted to get in.

And Sandra was a member. The most natural thing in the world would be for Sandra to nominate Jean at the next meeting. Someone else would second her, and Sandra was sure Jeannie would make it through the pledge period and be admitted to Pi Beta Alpha.

"Hey," she said quickly, cutting Jean off. "I forgot to tell Robin I can't make practice tomorrow. I'll be back in a second, OK?"

"OK," Jean said agreeably, watching her bound off.

What's wrong with me? Sandra asked herself, hurrying over to Robin's side. *Jean's my best friend. So why don't I want her to get into Pi Beta Alpha?*

"Congratulations, Amy!" Elizabeth cried, running over to her friend.

Amy looked overjoyed. "Just a sec, Liz," she said. "I just want to talk to Robin and Jess for a minute."

Elizabeth watched her hurry off. She was glad for Amy, but a tiny voice inside her reminded her that now Amy would be spending more time than ever with Jessica and the cheerleading crowd.

Stop it! Elizabeth told herself sharply. *You're being unbelievably childish. Amy doesn't have to prove anything to you. That's not what being a friend is all about!*

Taking a deep breath, Elizabeth crossed the grass to the spot where Amy was chatting with Jessica. "Amy," she called. "I'm about to take off, and I just want to ask you something, OK?"

Amy said something to Jessica that Elizabeth couldn't hear, and Jessica laughed. The next minute Amy joined Elizabeth, smiling.

"I'm so happy," she confided. "I really wanted to make the squad, Liz. Are you glad for me?"

"Absolutely," Elizabeth declared. "You were terrific, Amy. You really looked great."

"Thanks," Amy said, looking back over her shoulder at Jessica and Robin. "Liz, I sort of want to go over a few things with those guys before—"

Elizabeth bit her lip. "I'm meeting Enid at the mall now," she said rapidly, "and I just wanted to know if I could pick up a pair of ski gloves for you for this coming weekend. I remembered you said you didn't have any, right?"

Amy's gray eyes had a distant expression in them. "Right," she said absently.

"Should I get you a pair?" Elizabeth asked uncertainly. She had a feeling Amy hadn't really heard a word she'd said.

"What?" Amy asked, staring at her blankly. Then her pretty face cleared, and she smiled broadly. "Liz, you are *such* a doll!" she

69

exclaimed. "I'd love it if you'd pick me up some gloves. Now don't hate me, but I really do have to dash!" Seeing the downcast expression on Elizabeth's face, she added, "I'm so sorry, Liz. Let's meet at the Dairi Burger around five o'clock, OK?"

"OK," Elizabeth said halfheartedly. She sighed, watching Amy bounce back to join Jessica, Robin, and the other members of the squad.

All of a sudden Elizabeth wasn't looking forward to the ski weekend quite as much as she had been that morning. She was wondering what it was going to be like, having to stay in a cabin with Amy Sutton for three days. She wasn't one bit certain anymore that it was going to be fun.

Seven

Elizabeth put down the ski gloves she was looking at and began to giggle. "Enid," she whispered, tapping her friend gently on the arm. "Look at that couple over there!"

Enid followed her friend's gaze and chuckled. The middle-aged couple were staggering under mounds of packages. From the expressions on their faces, it was apparent they were in trouble. Things were slipping out of their arms, and any minute their expensive purchases were going to crash to the floor.

"Let's help them," Enid said, still smiling. Without a word Elizabeth crossed the floor of the brightly lit shop with her friend. Enid caught a ski pole just as it was about to fall, and Elizabeth grabbed an oversize package the woman was fumbling for.

"Thanks," the man said gratefully. He smiled sheepishly at his wife. "Guess you can tell we're not exactly experienced skiers."

Elizabeth fought hard to keep a straight face.

71

"Do you need some help carrying this stuff out to your car?" she asked politely.

The couple thanked them both but insisted they'd be able to manage. Watching the couple lug their loot to the door, Enid and Elizabeth exchanged merry glances. The minute the couple had vanished, the girls both doubled up with laughter.

"Did you see the look on her face?" Elizabeth asked weakly, wiping her eyes.

"They both looked so confused." Enid giggled. "Liz, do you think they're going to be up at Tahoe this weekend, too?"

Elizabeth shook her head, her blond ponytail swinging. "I hope not. We'd better take out special insurance if they are!"

"I know I've already said so a million times, but I just can't wait to get up there, Liz. We're going to have the best time!"

Elizabeth smiled. "We sure are. I'm excited about the weekend, too." Elizabeth didn't say it aloud, but she couldn't help the uneasy thought that crossed her mind. *I'd be even more excited if it were just going to be Enid and her aunt and me.* She couldn't remember the last time she had laughed so hard as she had just now with Enid. It felt like ages! But it had been only weeks, she told herself. Since before Amy moved in.

A few minutes later Elizabeth began to regret her negative feelings about Amy. *What kind of friend am I, anyway?* she reprimanded herself, heading back to the counter and picking up the gloves she had been looking at.

"I think I'm going to get these," Enid said, picking up a pair of navy quilted gloves filled with goose down. "They're on sale, too."

Elizabeth nodded, then looked closely at a pair of lipstick-red gloves she had spotted on the counter. They weren't as practical as the navy ones. She knew that they would get dirty much more quickly, and they were almost twice the price of the gloves Enid had picked out. "Do you think Amy would like these?" she asked tentatively, showing them to Enid.

Enid thought for a moment. "Yes," she said judiciously. "They look like her color."

Elizabeth nodded. "She really likes bright things. I'll take them," she decided quickly, "and I'll get a pair of the navy ones for myself."

Ten minutes later the girls were standing in the bright sunlight outside the shop. "Why don't you leave your car here and come to the Dairi Burger with me?" Elizabeth suggested, slipping her sunglasses on and checking her watch. "We can have a shake or a Coke or something, and then I'll drive you back here."

"Sounds kind of tempting," Enid said, her eyes brightening.

"I told Amy I'd meet her at five o'clock," Elizabeth added. "I'm sure she'd love it if you came, too."

Enid looked down at the ground. "I'd love to,

Liz, but I've got tons of homework tonight. Besides, I promised my mom I'd make dinner. I'd better just go straight home."

Elizabeth glanced away. Was it her imagination, or had Enid's expression changed the moment she had mentioned Amy's name? "Come on," she pleaded, putting her hand on her friend's arm. "We won't be long. I promise!"

Enid shook her head firmly. "Honestly, I can't," she repeated. She was quiet for a minute before meeting Elizabeth's gaze. "Did Amy make the squad?" she asked, a strange expression on her face.

Elizabeth nodded. "She was great," she said warmly. "It was clear right from the start that she was the best candidate."

Enid smiled. "Well, tell her I said congratulations, OK? And now I'd really better run, or my mom's going to kill me!"

Elizabeth sighed as she watched her friend hurry away. She couldn't suppress her feeling of uneasiness anymore.

Would Enid have joined her at the Dairi Burger, Elizabeth wondered, if Amy weren't going to be there? She had a feeling that the answer to that question was *yes*.

"Amy," Elizabeth protested weakly. "I don't want to be a spoilsport, but I've got to get home. Are you almost through?"

Elizabeth was upstairs in Amy's bedroom, trying to hold still while Amy put makeup on Elizabeth's eyes—the last touch to the make-over she had been intent on for the last fifteen minutes.

This wasn't exactly what Elizabeth had planned for the afternoon, and she was glad now that Enid hadn't come along. No sooner had she arrived at the Dairi Burger than she'd found Amy waiting for her outside, a look of impatience on her pretty face. "Where've you been?" she'd complained, jumping right into the car.

Elizabeth had stared at her, astonished. "I was with Enid at the mall. We were getting ski gloves for the trip, remember?"

Amy frowned. "I've been waiting for *ages*. Liz, be a doll and give me a ride home, will you? Johnny's supposed to call at five-thirty, and if I miss him I'll just die!"

Elizabeth bit her lip. "I thought I was meeting you here so we could get a soda—not so I could drive you home."

Amy smiled at her prettily. "I know that, Liz! Honestly, do you think I'm a total monster?"

Elizabeth just stared at her, then reluctantly turned the key in the ignition.

"It's just that I forgot all about John's phone call," Amy purred. "That's why I've been going so crazy out here! It suddenly crossed my mind that you and I would have more fun just going over to my house and catching up on things. And that way when John calls I'll be there!"

"OK," Elizabeth said wearily. If she had known that Amy's notion of "catching up on things" was going to consist of rattling on endlessly about cheerleading and glopping makeup all over her, Elizabeth might have thought twice before going with Amy to her house.

"You see," Amy was saying, stepping back and looking at Elizabeth critically, "all you needed was a bit more—*color*—"

She turned Elizabeth toward the mirror in the bedroom so she could get a look at herself. Elizabeth took a deep breath. "Isn't it a little dark for daytime?" she asked, resisting the urge to wipe her eyelids off then and there. She couldn't believe that was her own face staring back at her from the mirror. She looked so peculiar! Red lips, bright pink cheeks, lashes so thick and dark they looked fake.

"Well, you might not want it for every day," Amy admitted. "But for special occasions—"

That was all she could get out. The next instant the phone rang, stopping her in midsentence. "That's Johnny now!" Amy shrieked, rushing for the phone.

Elizabeth stared uneasily at her own reflection. She thought this was probably a good time to leave. Then she remembered she hadn't given Amy the ski gloves she'd bought at the mall. The package was still lying on Amy's bed, where

Elizabeth had dropped it when they came upstairs.

While she was waiting for Amy to come back, Elizabeth walked slowly around the room, looking at the snapshots and souvenirs covering the big cork bulletin board on the wall over Amy's bed. She guessed the tall, blond boy in the largest snapshot must be John Norton, but there were lots of pictures of other guys, most with their arms wrapped around Amy's waist or slung casually around her shoulders. There was a certain similarity about the pictures, though Elizabeth couldn't quite figure out what it was.

She couldn't help thinking how unlike Amy's old bedroom this was. No sports trophies, no medals for baton twirling, nothing to prove Amy had any interests in anything but boys, Elizabeth thought sadly. A pile of fashion magazines poked out from under the bed, and the half-open closet revealed a tangle of clothes that could rival the mess in Jessica's closet. Elizabeth went over to the mirror and wiped off a bit of the eyeshadow that Amy had applied. She couldn't wait to get home and wash her face.

A few minutes later Amy bounced back into the room, her face lit up with excitement. "He is just *dying*," she announced. "That's how much he misses me. He said—"

"Amy," Elizabeth cut in gently. "I really have to run. I just wanted to give you these before I left," she added, handing Amy the bag from the Ski Shop.

Amy's eyes sparkled as she pulled out the gloves. "Red!" she exclaimed. "My favorite color! Thanks, Liz. You're a doll. How much were they?"

Elizabeth smiled. "They're a present, silly. I wouldn't dream of letting you pay me."

Amy slipped one hand into a glove, then held it up admiringly. "Gee, thanks, Liz," she repeated. "That's awfully sweet of you."

"I hope you won't be too busy with cheerleading and everything to get away this weekend," Elizabeth said, smiling. "Let me know if I can do anything else to help you out before we go, OK?" She picked up her shoulder bag, ready to leave.

Pulling her hand out of the glove, Amy stared at Elizabeth. "*This* weekend?" she repeated incredulously. "But—"

Elizabeth felt a warning bell go off in her head. "What is it?" she demanded. "We've already set everything up, Amy. What's the problem?"

Amy blinked. "Well, it's just that Lila's party is this weekend. Liz, we can't go away and miss the biggest party of the whole *year*!"

Elizabeth felt immensely relieved. "Oh, is that all. I thought something was really wrong. Good heavens, Amy, Lila has a party practically every month. There'll be others. And the ski weekend is going to be really special."

Amy didn't say anything for a minute. "The thing is," she began finally, "I really feel like I *ought* to go to Lila's. I mean, it's really important when you're new to meet all sorts of interesting people. And her cousin Christopher—"

Elizabeth felt herself getting angry. "But you agreed to come this weekend!" she cried. "Why are you changing your mind now?"

Amy paled at the anger in Elizabeth's voice. "I'm sorry," she said, looking as though she might dissolve into tears. "But I didn't even *know* Lila before! Now that I know what a doll she is—"

Elizabeth frowned. "You two never had much in common before, did you?" she demanded.

Amy shrugged. "We were just kids then, Liz." Suddenly her expression became hopeful. "Couldn't you just ask Enid if we could go next weekend instead? Oh, Liz, *please!*"

Elizabeth looked away. She didn't know what to say. "We've already put the weekend off once, as it is," she said, feeling miserable. "We can't keep doing this to Enid's aunt. It isn't fair."

Amy put her hand beseechingly on Elizabeth's arm. "Liz, do me this one favor, and I promise I'll never ask you for anything again as long as I live," she said passionately. "Please, Liz! I want to go to Lila's party more than anything in the whole world!"

Elizabeth sighed. "Well, maybe I could try to

79

talk to Enid," she mumbled, staring at the carpet. "But—"

"Thank you!" Amy shrieked dramatically. "Oh, Liz, thank you! I promise," she added earnestly, "you won't be sorry!"

I don't know about that, Elizabeth thought grimly as she headed for the door.

The truth was that she was sorry already. And she hadn't the faintest idea what she was going to tell Enid.

Jessica was looking with satisfaction at the letter she had just finished writing to Miss Lovelorn. "This ought to do it," she said aloud, shaking her head with admiration as she reread the finished piece. "Perfect," she congratulated herself. Now that she had gotten to know Jay a little better, she knew all sorts of personal hints to add to make the letter more authentic. It was bound to hit close enough to home to start some good fights! She knew it would make Denise Hadley furious.

"Jess, can't you do that somewhere else? I'm trying to set the table," Elizabeth grumbled, thumping down four plates with a frown.

Jessica jumped, her reverie broken. "What's eating you?" she demanded, seeing the irate expression on her twin's face. "You look like you're about to clobber someone, Liz."

"I am," Elizabeth told her, arranging the silverware. "This feels like the longest day in history!"

"Look who's grumbling about long days!" Jessica retorted. "Who had to audition all those cheerleaders today, you or me?"

Elizabeth didn't answer. Thinking of the cheerleading tryouts made her feel worse than ever.

"Come on," Jessica said. "Tell me what's wrong. It helps to talk about it," she added sweetly. "That's what Miss Lovelorn always says."

Elizabeth glared at her. "If you really want to know," she said tersely, "Amy Sutton is what's wrong." Taking a deep breath, she proceeded to tell her twin all about the events of the afternoon. "What am I supposed to tell Enid now?" she concluded. "Either I'm a rat to Enid or a rat to Amy. I just don't know what to do!"

Jessica stared at her. "Is that all?" she asked lightly, folding the letter she had written and slipping it in her notebook. "Liz, that doesn't sound like much of a conflict to me."

"What do you mean?"

"Look," Jessica said earnestly. "Amy's absolutely right. So she agreed to go skiing with you and Enid before she'd even been back here a day or two! She needs to get her feet on the ground. You're not being fair. Can you blame her for wanting to go to the party?"

"I guess not," Elizabeth admitted.

"It's not as if Amy were trying to get out of the ski trip altogether," Jessica pointed out. "Which," she added, "would be a perfectly reasonable thing to do, if you ask me."

Elizabeth frowned.

"I'm serious, Liz. She's obviously eager to go with you guys, but naturally she wants to go to Lila's party. It's going to be a terrific bash, you know. It wouldn't hurt you and Enid to show up, either."

"I guess I can understand about the party," Elizabeth said slowly. "Amy could've just told us to go ahead without her. She obviously *does* still want to come."

Jessica nodded her head, her aqua eyes flashing. "And I think that's incredibly generous of her, considering how cruel Enid's being."

Elizabeth stared at her. "What are you talking about? Enid hasn't been cruel to Amy."

"Hah!" Jessica exploded. "*I* think she has. You're just too prejudiced. You can't even see what's going on right in front of you. Enid's jealous of Amy, and she's refusing to give her a chance. If you ask me, she's being a complete and total pain. And Amy's been so sweet and good-natured about it . . ."

Elizabeth bit her lip. She thought about the expression on Enid's face that afternoon when she had said she couldn't go to the Dairi Burger. Was Jessica right? Was Enid really jealous of

Amy, so jealous that she was actually hurting the other girl's feelings?

"Maybe it wouldn't be the end of the world to ask Enid to put the ski trip off one more weekend," Elizabeth said slowly, taking four glasses out of the cupboard and setting them down on the table.

Jessica flashed her sister her most sincere and helpful smile. Personally, she didn't think it would be the end of the world for Elizabeth to ask Enid to get lost once and for all. That Enid Rollins was a total zero in the personality department, Jessica thought.

She wasn't going to sit by and watch her very own twin do something as stupid as risk angering the glamorous and exciting Amy Sutton for someone as dull and dependable as Enid!

She has Amy now, Jessica reminded herself. *She doesn't need Enid Rollins any more!*

Eight

"Enid," Elizabeth said tentatively, unwrapping her roast beef sandwich, "I have a huge favor to ask you. Promise not to get mad at me, OK?"

The two girls were eating lunch at one of the small tables on the patio outside the cafeteria. It was the first opportunity Elizabeth had found to broach the subject of the upcoming weekend. And despite what Jessica had told her the previous night, she couldn't help feeling apprehensive.

"What is it?" Enid asked, concerned. "You look kind of upset, Liz. What's on your mind?"

Elizabeth sighed and put down her sandwich. "It's this weekend, Enid." She bit her lip, wondering which words to choose. But one look at her friend's face assured her that the direct approach was best. "Amy feels she really ought to go to Lila's party. I guess when she agreed to come along with us this weekend, she didn't really understand what she'd be missing."

"Oh," Enid said, her face unhappy. "I see."

"The thing is," Elizabeth added hastily, "she really does want to come along with us. She can't bear the thought of missing the weekend, so she asked me if I could ask you—"

"To cancel on my aunt again," Enid said shortly. "Right?"

Elizabeth felt terrible. "Enid," she said warmly, "please don't get angry about it! I mean, the girl's got a point. Hard as it is for me to understand what's so appealing about one of Lila's parties, I can see how she'd want to meet as many new people as possible."

"Liz," Enid said, pushing her salad away, "why don't we go up to Tahoe anyway? Just you and me?"

Elizabeth didn't say anything for a minute. "But Amy—"

"After all," Enid cut in, "you and I planned this trip before we even knew Amy was coming back. We could always go again sometime," she added, "and invite Amy to join us then. I hate the thought of putting Aunt Nancy to any more trouble. I know she'd never admit as much, but she's had to juggle her plans for the last few weeks just trying to accommodate herself to our last-minute changes."

Elizabeth felt terrible. She knew Enid was right. It was terribly rude to cancel on her aunt again, and it was wrong of Elizabeth to put her friend on the spot this way. Clearly Enid wanted to go ahead as planned.

But Elizabeth couldn't shake the feeling that she would be hurting Amy if she went up to Lake Tahoe that weekend with Enid and left Amy behind. Many things hadn't been as spectacular between her old friend and herself as she'd hoped, but Elizabeth was convinced she owed it to Amy to keep on trying. If she went on the trip with Enid and left Amy behind, it might be the final straw. Elizabeth just couldn't bear the thought of destroying what was left of their old friendship.

"Enid," she said, "I know exactly how you feel. In fact," she admitted, staring at her hands, "I know what I'm asking you to do is wrong." As briefly as possible, she explained her feelings. Enid listened without interrupting.

"OK," she said finally, her voice flat. "If that's what you really want, Liz, then that's what we'll do. But on one condition, OK?"

Elizabeth felt like jumping up and hugging her friend. "Whatever you say, Enid."

"Just that we pick a weekend now and stick to it, no matter what. Because when I call Aunt Nancy tonight I want to be able to assure her that this won't happen again."

"Next weekend," Elizabeth promised, "we'll go up to Tahoe, no matter what. How's that?"

Enid toyed with her fork. "That's fine," she said, her voice still slightly unnatural. "But, Liz—"

Elizabeth waited expectantly.

"I just hope Amy's really worth all this," Enid said uneasily, not meeting Elizabeth's gaze.

Elizabeth frowned as she picked up her sandwich. "That's not a very nice thing to say," she said quickly, wishing she had more ground to stand on in Amy's defense.

Enid remained quiet. She didn't know what to say. Her worst fears were confirmed, and it seemed whatever she did she could only get herself in deeper and deeper. She didn't like Amy Sutton, and it was getting harder and harder to conceal that from Elizabeth. Even worse, she suspected Elizabeth was growing disenchanted with her old friend as well but for some reason wouldn't admit it.

It hurt Enid more than she could say to feel Elizabeth pulling away from her like this. But she had promised herself she was going to stand by Elizabeth no matter what. She was holding to that promise, even though it was proving a whole lot harder than she had ever expected.

Jessica paused for a minute in the crowded cafeteria, taking a deep breath and running her fingers through her hair. "Here goes nothing," she whispered to herself as she headed across the room to the table where Jay McGuire was eating his lunch—by himself.

"Hi, Jay," she said casually, trying to sound as

though she had fallen into the seat across from him by pure chance.

"Hi," Jay said moodily. He was as gorgeous as ever, Jessica noticed, but he sure didn't look very happy. She wondered if her scheme to get Denise and him quarreling had worked.

"Where's Denise?" she asked brightly.

Jay sighed. "Who knows. I haven't seen her since yesterday. We're not really getting along very well lately," he added.

Jessica's eyebrows shot up. "That's terrible," she said sympathetically, inching over so her hand, lying casually on the table, was practically touching Jay's arm. "What's wrong? Or am I being too nosy?"

"No, that's OK," Jay mumbled. "The thing is, she's suddenly convinced that we're wrong for each other. Like one little year really makes a big difference," he added, looking miserable. "It's crazy! Suddenly she's all worried about things like what's going to happen next year when she's away at college and I'm still here."

Jessica frowned. "Sounds to me like she's hunting for an excuse to call things off. She doesn't deserve you, Jay."

"Yeah," Jay said sourly. "Maybe you're right, Jess. The way she's been carrying on—"

"I sure hope our column didn't have anything to do with this," Jessica said, watching Jay carefully. "In fact, it's a pretty strange coincidence. Did you read 'Miss Lovelorn' last week?"

Jay nodded gloomily. "Yeah. That's what started the whole thing."

Jessica's expression was pure theatrical dismay. "Oh, no!" she exclaimed, putting her hand on his arm. "Jay, I feel terrible! And the weird thing is, Cara and I really deliberated for *hours* about those letters. But in the end—"

"Oh, don't worry about it, Jess," Jay said, glancing down at her hand with some surprise. "I mean, you two were only doing your job. Who knows," he added. "Maybe there's some truth in what you two said. A few weeks ago I wouldn't have believed it, but from Denise's reaction—"

"It's true," Jessica said firmly. "Honestly, Jay, the fights you're having now just prove you two are mismatched! Believe me, you'll be better off without her."

Jay grimaced. "I sure don't feel any better off. In fact, I feel pretty lousy."

"You need to keep busy," Jessica said judiciously. "It isn't going to do you one bit of good to just sit around moping. What are you doing this Friday night, for example?" she asked, tightening her hand on his forearm.

Jay looked at her. "Nothing," he said. "Why?"

"Well . . ." Jessica said, lowering her lashes, "I was just thinking that maybe you and I could go out somewhere. You know, just to get a hamburger or something."

Jay shrugged. "I don't see why not," he said,

pulling his arm away. "I mean, if you really want to—"

"Great!" Jessica cried, bouncing to her feet. "Then it's a date. Why don't you come pick me up around eight?"

"Sure," Jay said, balling up his lunch bag and throwing it easily into the bin several yards away.

Jessica gave him her most winning smile as she hurried away to tell Lila and Cara the wonderful news. She was positive now that she would be able to convince Jay to be her date for Lila's party. And once she danced in his arms she knew he'd be hers completely.

Jessica had been planning her costume for weeks now, and she was convinced it was going to be the best one there. She was going to the party dressed as Cleopatra, one of the most enticing and beautiful women who'd ever lived. She was going to wear a white sheet, wound around her to make a long skirt, and a gold bandeau top that revealed her tan midriff and shoulders. With dark eye makeup and some exotic jewelry, Jessica knew she would look absolutely stunning. Jay would never know what hit him!

First, though, she had to get him to Lila's party. That meant Friday night she was going to have to do some pretty serious convincing—or Cleopatra would go to the biggest party of the year all by herself!

*　　*　　*

"Amy!" Elizabeth called, unable to hide the note of annoyance creeping into her voice. Amy was several yards in front of her in the congested main hallway, apparently oblivious to Elizabeth's rising voice. *"Amy!"* she tried once more.

The blonde swung around, gray eyes wide with innocent surprise. "Liz? Have you been calling me? Honestly, I'm in such a daze I can't even hear myself think! I've just got so much to do—all this cheerleading stuff and on top of all that, Cara and Lila are trying to get me to pledge their sorority, you know, Pi Beta Alpha, and—"

Pi Beta Alpha had just announced that the new pledging season would begin a week from Monday. To get into the sorority a pledge had to be nominated and seconded by a member, fulfill all the conditions of the pledge period, and then be voted in unanimously by the entire sorority. Amy Sutton had decided she wanted to get in more than anything in the world.

"Yes," Elizabeth interrupted dryly, "I know. But I also know we were supposed to get together for lunch again today. Today is Wednesday, remember?"

Amy snapped her fingers. "Gosh, I knew there was something I'd forgotten! Oh, Liz, I feel terrible! I was going to meet you, but Cara said—"

"Amy," Elizabeth said, squaring off and facing her friend with a determined look on her face, "this is the second lunch date you've broken. It just isn't fair! Don't you think *my* time counts, too?"

Amy's gray eyes filled with tears. "Of course it does," she said unhappily. "Oh, Liz, I could just kill myself I feel so terrible. The thing is, I've just gotten so overextended. I barely even have time to eat lunch anymore myself. I guess I've just been so excited about being in a new school that I've tried to do too much. Promise you'll forgive me," she added breathlessly. "Please promise, Liz. Honestly, when you look mad at me the way you do right now, I feel like I'm just going to crumble!"

Elizabeth laughed despite herself. "OK," she relented. "I forgive you. But you've got to keep your promises, too! Otherwise—"

"I will, I will," Amy said, her expression changing as rapidly as the sky after a summer storm. "I have so much to tell you, Liz. You won't believe it. I'm in love!"

Elizabeth laughed. "Did Johnny call again?"

Amy screwed her face up. "Not *Johnny*," she said scornfully. "I mean, he was OK and everything, but it was just stupid kid stuff. Nothing real. But this guy—"

Elizabeth looked at her. "Who's the lucky man this time?" she asked dryly. She couldn't help thinking that Amy sounded an awful lot like Jessica right now. More than Elizabeth cared to admit, in fact.

"Christopher," Amy breathed. "Lila's cousin.

He's *gorgeous*! I mean it. He's like a dream come true. Blond hair that's really thick and curly so you just want to run your fingers through it. And a fabulous tan, with the most adorable little freckles on the bridge of his nose. And his smile—"

"Amy," Elizabeth cut in, "I thought Christopher was in L.A. until the day of the party. Did he come back early or something? How'd you meet him?"

Amy looked defensive. "I haven't *met* him," she admitted. "But Lila's shown me dozens of pictures. And I really feel like I know him, too," she added when Elizabeth started to laugh. "Honestly, Liz! You don't have to actually *talk* to someone to know it's true love, do you?"

Elizabeth didn't answer. She didn't get a chance.

"Besides," Amy went on, "Lila really wants us to get together. She told me so herself. She thinks we'll make a terrific couple. And with her help . . ."

"I hope it works out," Elizabeth said sincerely, thinking privately that the last person she'd ever want involved with her love life would be Lila Fowler. "Anyway, it should make Saturday night more suspenseful for you, if nothing else!"

"Saturday night," Amy said dreamily, "is going to be the happiest night of my entire life!"

Nine

"Now," Jessica said, linking her arm through Jay's and smiling flirtatiously, "wasn't that a lot more fun than sitting at home and moping?"

"Yeah," Jay said dully, "I guess so."

Jessica ignored the flat sound of his voice. It was a beautiful, starlit night, perfect for romance. She and Jay had just come out of the Valley Cinema. They had eaten earlier at the Box Tree Café, a popular restaurant in town. The way Jessica saw it, the rest of the evening was free—and she had a pretty good idea where she wanted to spend it.

"Let's go up to Miller's Point," she said impulsively, as if the thought had just occurred to her.

Jay looked a little embarrassed. "Wouldn't you rather go over to the Beach Disco? Eddie and Tom said they were going to be there later on. We could meet them."

Jessica tossed her hair back with a patient smile. Eddie May and Tom Richardson were good friends of Jay's. Jessica thought that they were nice guys, but she had no intention of sharing Jay with them.

"I'd rather be alone with you, Jay," she said huskily, tilting her face up to stare meaningfully into his eyes. "We really haven't had any time to—you know, *talk*. We barely know each other."

"Yeah, I know," Jay said, stuffing his hands in his pockets. "OK," he said at last, pulling out the keys to his car. "Let's go if you really want to. But I promised my dad I'd have the car home early."

Jessica ignored the warning note in his voice. Fine, so Jay wanted to play things cool tonight, Jessica thought. That was OK with her. She was convinced she had Jay exactly where she wanted him. She had seen the way he was looking at her in the darkened movie theater.

Jessica had outdone herself that night. Her denim skirt was so short that it made her long, tanned legs appear to go on forever. The simple T-shirt and cotton scarf she wore to complete the outfit made a winning combination—simple, but sexy at the same time. She had even dabbed some of her mother's best perfume behind her ears and on her wrists. It smelled great—really warm and sultry. Jessica was sure Jay had noticed it.

Twenty minutes later the two of them were parked at Miller's Point, the grassy overhang looking out over the entire valley. Jay turned the engine of his father's Camaro off and switched off the headlights. The lights of the valley spread out before them.

"What a beautiful evening!" Jessica exclaimed, sliding across the seat and snuggling up to Jay. She lowered her eyes, afraid to look up at him. "I'm so happy to be up here with you," she said softly, putting her hand on his knee.

Jay jerked away, an expression of pain crossing his face. "Jess, don't," he said abruptly. "I knew it," he added a minute later. "I should never have come up here with you."

Jessica was quiet for a minute. "Are you thinking about Denise?" she asked at last.

Jay nodded. "Look, I'm sorry," he told her. "But I just can't get her off my mind. Whatever kind of crazy misunderstanding we've had will blow over. It's got to, Jess. When you're really in love . . ."

Jessica bit her lip. This didn't sound good at all. It was time for some drastic measures to be taken. "Jay," she said, thinking fast, "you've got to forget Denise. For your own good."

"Why?" Jay cried. "Jess, do you know something? Are you keeping something from me?"

"Well . . ." Jessica sighed. "I really didn't want to be the one to have to tell you, Jay, because as you can probably tell, I really like you a lot. But the truth's going to come out sooner or later. Denise has been seeing some guy behind your back. A lot of people at school know, only everyone was afraid to tell you."

"You're kidding," Jay said dully. "You mean—"

"I didn't want to be the one to tell you," Jessica said huskily, rubbing his shoulder to show how sympathetic she felt. She felt a tiny twinge of guilt about her lie, since Jay looked crushed. But deep down she was convinced it was all for the best. She really did believe that he and Denise were wrong for each other. And if it took a little white lie to help him see that, then—

"I haven't been very friendly to you tonight, Jess," Jay said suddenly, looking at her with a new expression in his eyes. "Why've you been putting up with me, anyway?"

Jessica blushed. "I like—putting up with you," she murmured. "If you ever do forget about Denise and decide you'd like to get to know someone new. . . ." She let her voice trail off, looking at him through lowered lashes.

Jay leaned over and ran his hand along her smooth jaw. "What about right now?" he whispered, drawing her face up toward his.

Jessica closed her eyes, her heart racing as his warm lips touched hers.

Right now, she told herself deliriously, was just about the best time she could possibly have imagined!

*   *   *

Elizabeth was sitting downstairs in the Wakefields' comfortable living room, an unread novel open on the couch beside her. The house was quiet, but she barely noticed. She was thinking.

It wasn't as if Elizabeth had planned to spend Friday night alone at home. As a matter of fact, she had been counting on going out and having a good time. But Amy had stood her up—again. And this time, Elizabeth felt as though she had really had it.

The strange thing was that it had been Amy's idea to go see an old movie at the Plaza that night. She had called the night before, and she and Elizabeth had had the best talk since Amy had moved. Amy apologized for missing their lunch dates and said she really didn't know what was wrong with her, why she'd been so inconsiderate. She went on and on about how sorry she was that she'd seen so little of Elizabeth. Elizabeth was completely won over by their talk. When Amy begged her to go to the movies with her, Elizabeth was delighted to say yes. Amy said she'd be over at eight.

By eight-fifteen Elizabeth was pacing up and down, wondering what could have gone wrong. She found herself making all sorts of excuses for Amy: the car wouldn't start; she had to run an errand for her mother; she'd gotten lost or something and would be over any minute. By eight-thirty Elizabeth had run out of excuses. She called the Suttons' house four times, but no one answered. Wherever Amy was, they had missed the movie. And Elizabeth had to face facts. Amy Sutton just couldn't be depended on.

For the next hour Elizabeth had sat curled up on the couch, thinking over the events of the past few weeks. Her parents were out at a charity dinner, and Jessica was out with Jay, so she had plenty of peace and quiet in which to ruminate.

The more Elizabeth thought about the situation, the more convinced she was that Amy had changed. She could see now how blind she had been to the girl's inconsiderate behavior. And try as she might to defend herself for being generous and forgiving, she knew her blindness had hurt Enid very badly.

Hadn't she been as inconsiderate to Enid as Amy had been to her? One by one she ticked off the times over the last few weeks that she'd stood Enid up or broken dates with her. Because of Elizabeth, Enid had had to cancel their ski weekend *twice*. Elizabeth had put her through the pain and embarrassment of having to back out of their plans and explain everything to her aunt. She had expected Enid to be forgiving— just as Amy expected *her* to be forgiving. Had she been taking advantage of Enid's friendship?

Suddenly Elizabeth felt terrible. She just hoped it wasn't too late to tell Enid how she felt! Crossing the room in a few quick strides, she picked up the receiver and dialed Enid's number. After several rings, Mrs. Rollins answered the phone. "Elizabeth!" she exclaimed. "I haven't seen you in ages."

Elizabeth bit her lip guiltily. Even Enid's mother had noticed her absence. "Is Enid home?" she asked hopefully.

"No, dear," Mrs. Rollins said apologetically. "She's gone out with a whole bunch of kids. I'm not sure where. Funny," she added, "I just assumed you'd be with them."

"Well, just tell her I called, OK?" Elizabeth asked. A lump formed in her throat as she hung up the phone.

Everything seemed so complicated all of a sudden! She wandered forlornly over to the sliding glass door to the patio and pool. She just didn't feel like reading her novel or watching TV. The truth was, she felt kind of lonely.

She was still standing at the door, looking outside and thinking, when the door bell rang several minutes later. It was Amy, her blond hair perfectly arranged, as usual, and her hands gesturing wildly as the words tumbled out. "I'm so sorry!" she cried as she hurried into the front hallway. "You must be furious with me, and I don't blame you a bit. But you'll never in a million years guess what happened to me. I swear to God you won't."

Elizabeth looked at her skeptically. "What

happened?" she asked. She couldn't help thinking, *This had better be good*.

Amy took a deep breath and launched into a story that took so long to tell that Elizabeth wasn't surprised it made Amy late. Ten minutes later she was still breathlessly racing along. First her mother had asked her to be an angel and dash over to Season's Gourmet Shop to get some mint sauce because they suddenly decided at the station that she should have a dinner party. And then the guests started arriving, and her mother was in the bathtub. So Amy had to entertain them. *Then* the car wouldn't start. Then—

Elizabeth looked incredulously at Amy while she went on and on. "If your mother's having a dinner party over at your house tonight, how come no one answered when I called about an hour ago?" she asked pointedly.

Amy looked startled. "They must've all been outside," she said. "That's where they're eating—out on the patio. And you can't hear the phone when the door's closed."

Elizabeth didn't know whether to believe Amy or not. Suddenly she realized that she desperately *wanted* to believe her. She didn't want to lose Amy's friendship. They had meant so much to each other when they were growing up. To lose Amy now would mean cutting out a part of her life that had meant a great deal to her. Elizabeth took a deep breath. "Do you want a Coke or something?" she asked tentatively.

"After all you've been through, you must be thirsty."

Amy smiled broadly. "I'd love one," she said enthusiastically. "Oh, Liz, I'm so glad you're not mad at me. I can't tell you how terrified I was, coming over here. I kept thinking, 'If she says she never wants to talk to me again, what am I going to do?'" Tears were shining in Amy's eyes. And she looked so sincere, so heartbreakingly sincere.

Elizabeth honestly didn't know what to think anymore.

Jessica hummed to herself as she opened the front door with her key. The house was dark. *Everyone must be asleep*, she thought. She tiptoed across the front hall to the staircase, flicking on a light and stopping at the mirror to look briefly at her reflection. She couldn't help giggling. She looked as though she'd had a good time. Her hair was all mussed up, and her eye makeup was smudged. Oh, well, she thought philosophically. Jay hadn't seemed to mind the way she looked. Not at all!

They had spent a good long time together up at Miller's Point. And by the time Jay dropped her off, he'd seemed like a completely different person. He'd seemed to have forgotten all about Denise Hadley—and Jessica certainly wasn't going to remind him!

The best moment of the evening came when Jay walked her to the door. "Hey," he said tenderly, nuzzling her ear a little, "how'd you like to come to Lila's party with me tomorrow night? If you're not already going with someone, I mean."

Jessica felt as if she were walking on air. "That would be really nice," she told him. She smiled up into his eyes. "I'd really like that."

So it was a date! Jessica could barely wait to assemble all the pieces of her Cleopatra costume. She knew Jay would love it. They were going to have such a fabulous time.

There was just one thing worrying Jessica now, and she wanted to take care of it before she went to sleep. A few days earlier she had found six letters in the "Miss Lovelorn" box in the *Oracle* office. Two were from sophomores, complaining that no one liked them. *How boring*, Jessica thought. But she couldn't believe her eyes when she read the third and fourth letters. One was signed "Heartbroken" and the other "Missing Her." They were like clones: saying how heartsick and sad they felt without the other and what a dumb misunderstanding they'd had. Jessica was sure the letters had come from Jay and Denise. She hadn't wanted to risk their ever being read by anyone else, so she had grabbed them and stuck them in her notebook. She would destroy them later, she thought. She wasn't going to risk a reunion between Jay and Denise.

Jessica opened her notebook now and sorted through the stray pieces of paper for the letters. To her dismay, she realized she had taken the letters from the sophomore girls instead. "Damn," Jessica said aloud. She must have left the other letters in the "Miss Lovelorn" box.

Well, she wasn't going to let it spoil this perfect weekend. She made a mental note to get to school early Monday morning and get the letters before anyone else saw them.

After all, Jessica told herself, that was what being an editor meant, keeping a sharp eye out for little slip-ups! and no little slip-up was going to sail past her, especially if it was one that might reunite the star-crossed lovers she had worked so hard to break up!

Ten

Elizabeth bit her lip as she critically inspected her reflection in her full-length mirror. She just wasn't that excited about Lila's party that night, and she had to admit her costume wasn't very original. She was dressed as a skier, in tight-fitting navy blue ski pants and a brightly striped turtleneck, with a pair of sunglasses pushed back high on her head. She was also carrying the ski gloves she had bought with Enid earlier in the week.

Though not unusual, Elizabeth's costume was meant to convey a special message to Enid. She wanted her friend to know she was thinking about the weekend in Lake Tahoe. She wanted Enid to know she was thinking about *her*—and she just hoped Enid understood. They had had another strained conversation earlier that evening, and once again the problem was because of Amy. Elizabeth had offered Enid a ride to the party days ago. They almost always went to things like this together if neither had a date. The problem arose early that afternoon, when Amy called up in hysterics. She couldn't borrow her mother's car. Could Elizabeth and Enid possibly squeeze her in the Fiat? Elizabeth said yes, never dreaming that Enid would be upset. But when she mentioned to Enid that they'd have an extra passenger along, Enid sounded far from thrilled. "Maybe I'll make other arrangements, in that case," she had said unhappily.

Elizabeth had felt like crying. "Enid, what is it with you two? Can't you just put up with Amy for a ten-minute car ride?"

Enid had been quiet for a minute. "Liz," she said finally, "you know I wouldn't hurt you for the world. Honestly. It's not a big thing. I'll get my mother to drop me off."

Elizabeth felt a pang, remembering what Enid had said weeks ago about three being a crowd.

She was beginning to understand what Enid meant. It struck Elizabeth now that she was being forced to choose between Enid and Amy. She couldn't understand how things had turned out so badly. Why was Enid being so difficult? Unless . . .

Well, unless what Jessica had told her was right. Unless Enid was so jealous of Amy that she couldn't bear to give her a chance.

Or unless Amy had done something so cruel to Enid that Enid just couldn't face her. But if the second possibility were true, Enid would surely have told her!

106

All of these thoughts were flying through Elizabeth's head as she got ready for Lila's party. Jessica, looking like a movie star in her flamboyant Cleopatra costume, had already left for the party with Jay McGuire. Elizabeth realized she was purposely stalling for time. She was almost dreading this evening, and she knew she had no reason to.

Or did she? she thought unhappily, heading downstairs. Maybe she really *was* justified in fearing that that night there was finally going to be a showdown between Amy and Enid.

If the uneasy sensation in her stomach was a fair warning sign, then the evening ahead was bound to be stormy. Elizabeth couldn't remember feeling so confused and upset. She had no idea anymore whose side she was on. All she knew was that sooner or later she was going to be forced to choose. And she had a distinct feeling that the moment was going to be sooner than she'd expected.

"How do I look?" Amy asked Liz for the dozenth time, fidgeting in the passenger seat to get another look at her hair.

"You look fine," Elizabeth said automatically. The truth was, Amy looked terrific. She was dressed as a ballerina. She was wearing a sparkling white tutu flecked with glitter, white tights, satin toe shoes, and a tiara. Big blond curls cascaded around her shoulders like spun gold, and the total effect was pure romance.

"I hope Christopher likes ballerinas," Amy said, readjusting her tiara and giggling nervously. Elizabeth pulled the Fiat up the long drive leading to Fowler Crest, the Fowlers' magnificent estate, located on the hill overlooking the valley. Cars were parked up and down the drive already, and Elizabeth couldn't get the Fiat very far. "Let's leave the car here," she said, expertly parking. Up ahead, one of the Fowlers' servants was standing in the cutout of light at the open front door, greeting guests and directing them through the front hall of the mansion to the garden. It was a spectacular evening, and despite herself Elizabeth began to get excited.

A few minutes later Amy and Elizabeth were standing in the Fowlers' majestic garden, each sipping a cold drink. Elizabeth looked around her in amazement. She could never understand how Lila found ways to outdo herself with each new party, but this time really seemed to be the ultimate. Lighted candles floated in glass bubbles in the large swimming pool, so the water seemed to glow like a sheet of moonlight. The rich scent of flowers laced the air. A long table covered with a snowy white tablecloth was heaped at one end with brownies, cookies, and cakes of every variety. Sodas and cold drinks were at the other end. On a raised dais, the Number One were setting up their instruments.

They were one of the most popular new bands in California, and Elizabeth still couldn't believe Mr. Fowler had gotten them to play there that night.

The most fun thing by far, though, was watching everyone show up in costume and trying to figure out who was who. Privately Elizabeth thought Jessica's costume was the most outstanding. Her gold top was as skimpy as a bathing suit, and the white sheet flowed majestically around her. She had even put glitter on her shoulders so they gleamed! Lila, who had come as the Princess of Wales, didn't look half as good, Elizabeth decided. She had had to ask who Lila was supposed to be. Cara Walker and Steven Wakefield, Elizabeth's brother, who had come home from college for the weekend, looked adorable as Raggedy Ann and Raggedy Andy. Winston Egbert was looking his usual comical self, wearing a bathing cap and enormous sunglasses, a plaid bathing suit, and rubber flippers. The rest of the costumes ranged from astronauts to sports heroes to caricatures of teachers at school. Several girls were dressed as rock stars or dancers, but as Amy pointed out with visible relief, she was the only ballerina.

Elizabeth began to chuckle when Amy told her that.

"What's so funny?" Amy demanded, looking around for Lila's cousin Christopher.

"Nothing," Elizabeth said. "It's just that I'm not the only skier here, that's all."

She had just seen Enid come through the open door into the garden. And Enid was dressed in almost the exact same outfit she was, down to the quilted, navy gloves!

"Excuse me a second," Elizabeth said to Amy, crossing the garden toward Enid. Enid's eyes lit up when she took in Elizabeth's costume.

"Liz!" She laughed and gave her friend an impulsive hug. "You dressed for Tahoe, too!"

Suddenly Elizabeth felt as though everything might be salvaged. "Great minds think alike," she said, hugging Enid back. "Hey," she added under her breath, "I'm sorry about the car ride. Forgive me?"

"Of course," Enid said, looking at Elizabeth as if she were daft. "Don't you realize I'm your *friend*?"

Something about Enid's voice made Elizabeth glow all over. "Hey," she said suddenly, "that must be Lila's mysterious cousin Christopher. Don't you think so?"

Enid stared. "Wow, Lila was really telling the truth. He's gorgeous," she said, her green eyes fixed on the tall, handsome young man walking with Lila toward the dais.

Lila grabbed the microphone the band had set up on the small wooden stage. "Hey, everybody!" she exclaimed. "Welcome!"

A burst of applause thundered around the

crowded garden. Lila put her hand up. "Thanks," she said. "But all I really want to say right now is to go ahead and eat, drink, dance, and be merry. But first, I want to introduce you to a very special person, who just happens to be the reason we're all here tonight. Everybody, this is my cousin Christopher!"

Wild applause greeted this introduction. Elizabeth had to admit Christopher was everything Lila had promised, at least as far as appearance went. He was about six foot two, with blond, wavy hair, and large blue eyes that twinkled as he surveyed the crowd. He really was handsome, Elizabeth thought. She nudged Enid. "He isn't wearing a costume," she pointed out.

Enid giggled. "Maybe he's supposed to be a prince, since Lila's supposed to be a princess."

Elizabeth smiled. "Hey," she said suddenly. "Prince Charming is staring at you, Enid. Maybe I should get out of your way so—"

"*Chris*," the girls overheard Lila saying in a low, urgent tone. "There's someone I really want you to meet. She's—"

"Just a minute, Lila," Christopher told her, still staring at Enid. "There's someone over here I've got to say hello to first. I'll be just a minute," he promised. The next minute he had crossed the crowded garden and was taking Enid's arm.

"Enid Rollins," he said warmly, a pleasant smile on his face. The next minute his eyes crinkled up with an expression of mock anguish.

111

"Don't tell me you've already forgotten me! And I thought I was the best sailing instructor ever to hit Camp Kennebunkport!"

Enid slapped her hand to her forehead. "Chris Hunter!" she exclaimed. "Good heavens. I had no idea you were Lila's cousin. When she said—"

The next minute the two were trading memories of the summer camp Enid had attended two years before, where Chris had headed waterfront activities. Elizabeth waited for an appropriate moment before slipping away. From the way the conversation was going, it looked as though Chris and Enid might prefer to be alone. "I *thought* you looked familiar," Elizabeth heard Enid saying happily, "but I never realized—"

Elizabeth grinned as she headed over to the table to choose from the mouth-watering array of desserts. Apparently Enid and Prince Charming were hitting it off just fine!

Elizabeth was delighted for Enid. And now that she knew Enid wasn't mad at her, she was ready to relax and enjoy the rest of the evening.

Jessica was in the powder room off the Fowlers' main hall, retouching the black kohl she had smudged around her eyes. She looked speculatively at herself in the mirror, adjusting the gold bandeau top. *Not bad*, she thought. *Not bad at all.* And from the way Jay McGuire kept looking at her, she was sure the costume was having the desired effect!

Just as Jessica was blending in a dab of brick-colored powder under her cheekbones, the door to the powder room swung open, and Amy and Lila burst in, talking furiously.

"I can't even *believe* her," Amy said, her face pale. She glanced at Jessica without a smile.

"What's going on?" Jessica demanded.

"It's Enid Rollins," Lila hissed. "She's made off with my cousin Christopher. And everyone knew he was supposed to be reserved for Amy!"

"I can't stand that girl," Amy seethed, catching sight of herself in the mirror and fluffing her mane of gold hair. "First she tries to steal Liz away from me. And now Chris!"

"Wait," Jessica said blankly, looking from Lila to Amy with complete confusion. "You mean Christopher actually likes *Enid*? Dull, plain, average old Enid Rollins?"

"Apparently," Lila said tersely, "he knows her from some sailing camp he used to teach at. And I guess they were sort of friendly then. Don't worry, Amy," she added quickly. "He's obviously just being polite to her—and she's monopolizing him. We'll get him away from her, and once he takes one look at you—"

"You think so?" Amy asked. "You think if I really *try*—"

"Good heavens," Jessica interjected with a sly smile, "if *I* managed to convince Jay to be my date tonight, Amy, you should be able to tear Chris away from Enid Rollins." She giggled. "Not really very stiff competition for you, is she?"

Amy began to look a little more like herself. "Well, he's probably bored stiff by now anyway. I guess the least I can do is go over and ask him to dance."

"That's the spirit!" Lila said with conviction. "Come on, Amy. Let's give this all we've got!"

Jessica followed the two girls out into the hall, a little smile playing about her lips. She had looked forward to this evening for such a long time, and now everything was going exactly as she'd planned. She caught sight of Jay, standing with two drinks in his hands, waiting for her, and a triumphant feeling washed over her. Jessica Wakefield had done it again!

"Jay," she said in her sultriest voice, reaching up for one of the Cokes he was holding. "Isn't it a gorgeous night?" She cuddled up close to him. "We're going to have so much *fun* tonight," she added, oblivious to the stormy expression on Jay's face.

"I wish you hadn't taken so long in there," he said shortly, setting his drink down. "Jess, I just wanted to tell you that I can't stand it here a minute longer. I'm leaving! If you want to come with me, fine. Otherwise—"

Jessica stared at him, her aqua eyes as big as saucers. "But, Jay, what's wrong? I thought—"

114

"That," Jay said, pointing across the garden, "is what's wrong."

Jessica followed his gaze. Denise Hadley, looking absolutely stunning in a long, glittering gown, was standing arm in arm with a young man Jessica didn't recognize. He looked a few years older.

"Don't worry about that," Jessica said quickly, tucking her arm through Jay's. "Let's just have a good time, you and me. Forget Denise."

Jay's expression darkened. "I can't stay here," he said, his voice tortured. "Jess, I'm sorry, but it hurts too much." His green eyes filled with tears, and he turned on his heel, storming out of the garden, leaving Jessica alone. She stared after him, too shocked to say a word.

"Looks like trouble," Cara Walker said, coming over to Jessica with a knowing look on her pretty face. "Did Miss Lovelorn's advice suddenly backfire?"

"Oh, shut up!" Jessica said furiously, racing away from Cara. Her perfect evening was ruined, totally, completely, utterly ruined. And the last person on earth she wanted sympathy from right now was Miss Cara Lovelorn Walker.

Enid took a deep breath, fighting for control. She couldn't believe this was happening to her.

The first part of the evening had been so much fun! It was great discovering Christopher was actually a friend. They had always liked each other, and Enid was pleased to find Christopher was as sincere and down to earth as ever. It was hard to believe he was really a relative of Lila's, in fact. They didn't really seem to have much in common. Christopher confided that he had escaped to L.A. because Lila got to be a bit much at times. Within minutes he and Enid were talking like intimates, joking about old times, trading opinions about the other guests, dancing and laughing together, and having a wonderful time. Enid felt ecstatic. And Chris wasn't acting like a big brother any more, either. He held her close when they danced, and Enid felt her heart begin to beat faster. . . .

And then the trouble began. Out of nowhere Amy Sutton appeared and asked Chris if he'd dance one tiny little dance with her. Chris had looked at Enid, a confused expression on his face. "Would you mind?" he asked her.

There was a lump in Enid's throat as she watched the two of them. Chris was bound to want to keep dancing with Amy, she thought miserably. Who could blame him? Amy was so beautiful. Enid wished that she'd worn something a little less athletic. Something prettier.

To her surprise Chris came right back after that one dance. "Back again," he said lightly, taking her in his arms. Enid felt the lump melt in her throat. But she was also aware, this time, that

Amy was watching them and glaring, her pretty face worked into an expression of wrath.

The rest of the evening was ruined for Enid. Amy followed her and Chris everywhere, interrupting their conversation, begging Chris to take her on a tour of the grounds, pleading for another dance, coming up with excuses to separate Enid and him at every turn. When Chris, looking exhausted, went up to the table to get Enid some dessert, Amy turned on her, her voice caustic. "Enid Rollins," she said, her eyes flashing fire, "didn't I tell you before just to get lost? Don't you know you make me sick?" She looked so angry Enid felt almost afraid. "I told you this last week: You can't steal people from me! I won't let you steal Liz, and I'm not going to let you steal Chris, either! He's mine," she said savagely, leaning closer. "He's mine, Enid. Now just stay away from him!"

Fighting for composure, Enid looked at her. "Amy, I told you before. I'm not going to make a scene with you. I care too much for Liz to do that. And Liz likes you," she added. "But Chris knows his own mind, Amy. You can't own people, however much you'd like to."

Amy spun on her heels, her eyes spilling over with angry tears. "I bet I can," she said with venom. "You just wait and see, Enid. You're going to be good and sorry. Chris won't ever talk to you again after tonight. And neither will Liz!"

And with that she stalked off, leaving Enid gaping.

Enid took a deep, shuddering breath. Whatever happened, Elizabeth couldn't find out, she told herself for the dozenth time. This wasn't the first time Amy Sutton had threatened her. But Enid had sworn to keep quiet at all costs.

It was up to Elizabeth to make up her own mind about Amy. And no matter how horrible she was to Enid, Enid was going to keep it to herself. For Elizabeth's sake.

But despite her promise to herself, Enid was beginning to run out of patience. She didn't know how much longer she'd be able to keep Amy Sutton's threats to herself.

"Enid," Elizabeth said, coming up to her friend, "do you need a lift home? I think I'm going now."

Enid shook her head. "Chris said earlier that he'd give me a ride," she said shyly.

Elizabeth chuckled. "A better offer than mine," she admitted. "You really like him, don't you?"

Enid nodded. "He's really nice. Only—" Her face darkened as she thought about Amy's threats. "I'm not sure he really likes me," she concluded lamely.

Elizabeth was about to answer when Amy ran up, out of breath. "Liz, I've got to talk to you for

118

a second," she said, tugging at Elizabeth's arm. "*Alone*," she added, glaring at Enid.

"Amy," Elizabeth said, surprised. "That wasn't very nice of you. What's Enid supposed to think?"

Amy had tugged her beyond Enid's earshot by now. "Listen," she said, ignoring Elizabeth's remonstrance, "I hope you won't be mad, but I'm not going to be coming home with you. Chris is driving me home."

"Chris?" Elizabeth said blankly. "But I thought—" Her eyes narrowed. "Amy," she said suddenly, "did you *ask* Chris to take you home, or did he just offer?"

Amy's eyes flashed. "Maybe I asked him, and maybe I didn't," she said shortly. "What's the difference? Honestly, Liz, you don't have to look at me that way!"

"I know for a fact that he was planning to give Enid a ride home," Elizabeth said firmly. "How'd you convince him to change his mind?"

Amy grinned. "I told him there wasn't enough room in your car. I convinced him I'd have to walk otherwise. Lucky for me, he's a real gentleman," she added. "Otherwise, my little scheme might have backfired."

Suddenly Elizabeth was angry. "That wasn't fair, Amy. You lied. Chris really likes Enid, and you're just—"

Amy put her hands over her ears. "I've had it," she fumed. "Do you realize all I've heard since the day I moved back is how terrific you think Enid is? Don't you realize"—her eyes flashed—"that I don't care? I think she's a total bore! And I'm sick and tired of having you try to ram her down my throat!"

Elizabeth stared at her, incredulous. "How can you *say* something like that?" she demanded. "Amy—"

The next minute Amy burst into tears. "Liz," she said miserably, "it isn't that I don't like Enid. She's all right. But I don't want to have to share you with her. Ever since I came back, I've wanted to recreate the friendship we had. And instead I find that you've already *got* a best friend. Enid! She's always in the way."

Still crying, Amy ran from the garden—smack into Chris, who said something to her, put his arm around her, and escorted her through the door. Elizabeth stood as still as a statue, not knowing what to think. The next minute Enid was beside her.

"Thanks a lot, Liz," Enid said coldly, watching Chris and Amy leave. "I guess you and Amy sure fixed *me*, huh?"

"What are you talking about?" Elizabeth cried.

"You went along with her," Enid spat out. "You let her tell him you didn't have room for her in your car."

Elizabeth shook her head. "Enid, I didn't know—" she began.

Enid was too angry to listen. "I've had it, Liz,"

she said shortly. "With both of you!" And the next minute Enid charged out of the garden. Elizabeth felt as though the world were crashing in around her. When she thought there might be trouble that evening, she had never expected this!

"Liz," a small, forlorn voice said at her shoulder, "I don't suppose I can squeeze into the Fiat?"

Elizabeth turned and looked at her twin, who looked like the saddest Cleopatra imaginable. She laughed bitterly. "You won't have to squeeze," she said shortly. "As a matter of fact, there's plenty of room."

"What happened to Amy and Enid?" Jessica asked, curiosity getting the better of her, even in her misery.

Elizabeth glared at her. "What happened to Jay?" she asked in response.

Linking arms, the twins went to say good night to Lila and thank her for the party. Neither could muster much enthusiasm. It was one of the worst nights either could remember in a long, long time.

Eleven

Elizabeth woke up Sunday morning feeling terrible. At first she couldn't remember what had gone wrong, and then it all came rushing back to her, as vividly and painfully as if she were experiencing it again as she had the previous night. Both Amy and Enid were furious with her. She had gone from feeling that she had to choose between two best friends to feeling that she'd lost them both!

It was eleven o'clock, and Elizabeth couldn't believe she'd been able to sleep so late. She knew it was only because she had spent most of the night tossing and turning, going over and over the events of Lila's party in her mind. By the time she had finally fallen asleep, the sun was coming up. No wonder she felt terrible now.

Swinging her legs over the side of her bed, Elizabeth reached for the telephone on her bedside table and pulled it into her lap. Before she could stop to think, she dialed Enid's number.

She wasn't going to feel better until she had righted things with her and Amy.

"Oh," Enid said, not sounding very excited. "It's you."

"Enid," Elizabeth said, "I want to apologize for our misunderstanding last night. I don't really know what happened, but I feel terrible! Can I come over? I think we need to talk."

"Sorry," Enid said abruptly, "but I'm doing errands for my mother today. Besides," she said curtly, "I don't really see what we have to talk about, Liz. I think you and I just have different ideas about things these days."

"Enid!" Elizabeth gasped. "Wait," she added desperately. "Don't hang up, OK?"

Enid didn't say anything, but Elizabeth could hear her breathing. She knew her friend hadn't hung up.

"Look," Elizabeth tried again, "I'm not sure exactly what's gone wrong, but I want to do what I can to help fix it. Please, Enid. You're the closest friend I have!"

"I don't know," Enid said, sounding tired and sad. "I wish I believed that, but that isn't really the way you've been acting, Liz."

Elizabeth didn't know what to say. Was Enid right?

"Listen," Enid added, "I feel bad about things, too. But right now. . . ." Her voice trailed off. "Why don't we just kind of cool off for a while," she said finally. "We can talk at school tomorrow or the next day."

"But—"

"I'm sorry, Liz," Enid said firmly. "I have to go now." And the next thing Elizabeth knew, Enid had hung up the phone.

Her heart beating quickly, Elizabeth dialed the Suttons' number. After about five rings Dyan Sutton picked up the phone. "Oh, hello, Liz," she said, sounding as friendly and poised as ever. "No, sweetie, I'm afraid Amy's not here. She went to the beach with Lila and Jessica."

"Oh," Elizabeth said in a small voice. "Thanks." *Lila and Jessica!* she thought furiously. She really felt as if she'd been left in the lurch now. And Jessica hadn't even woken her up to invite her to go along!

Elizabeth couldn't remember when she had felt so rotten. There was no denying it. She'd messed things up. Nothing had gone the way she had hoped it would.

Not only had Amy and Enid ended up disliking each other, they had both ended up disliking *her*!

Elizabeth felt like crawling back into bed and hiding under the covers all day. She didn't care if it was beautiful and sunny outside. She was convinced that there was nothing worth getting up for.

*　　*　　*

124

"OK," Alice Wakefield said, pouring herself a second cup of coffee. "Are you going to tell me why you're looking so glum, or am I supposed to be able to work it out by mental telepathy?"

Elizabeth tried to smile at her mother, but her facial muscles wouldn't work right. "Oh, Mom," she said finally, her face crumpling. "Everything's turned into such a terrible mess!"

Mrs. Wakefield regarded her daughter. "Sounds bad," she said, sitting down with Elizabeth at the table. "Anything your ancient mother can help you with, or would you rather bottle it all up and drive yourself crazy?"

Elizabeth took a deep, shaky breath. "It's Amy," she began, feeling terrible just thinking about the mess she was in. "And Enid. Mom, I'm afraid they're both going to hate me as long as I live!"

"OK," Mrs. Wakefield said, taking a sip of coffee. "Let's start at the beginning, can we?" She looked closely at Elizabeth. "I'm not sure when the beginning is, though. The day Amy moved in?"

Elizabeth shook her head helplessly. "I'm not sure either. At first things seemed perfectly simple. It was just a matter of introducing them and hoping they'd get along."

"But they didn't?" Mrs. Wakefield asked.

Elizabeth shook her head. "I guess not. But to be honest, I didn't really notice. Not right away. Not until—"

"Not until when?"

"Well, I didn't really notice until last night. I mean, I got the feeling before that they weren't one hundred percent excited about each other. But I didn't think they *hated* each other, either."

"What makes you think they hate each other?" Mrs. Wakefield asked, surprised.

Elizabeth began, bit by bit, to fill her mother in on the events of the past few weeks. She told her mother all about the ski trip, about Amy's excitement about Christopher, about Lila's party. "It kept coming to a showdown," she said, sighing, "between Amy and Enid. If Amy was coming along, Enid wouldn't join us."

"Honey," Mrs. Wakefield interjected, "from what you've told me, it sounds as though Amy's been changing your plans quite a bit. How many times did you say she stood you up at lunch?"

"Twice," Elizabeth admitted.

"Any other times she canceled out on you?"

"Well, we were supposed to go to the movies on Friday night, but she didn't show up until almost ten o'clock," Elizabeth sighed again. "The thing is, she's always so *apologetic* about these things. It makes me feel bad about getting angry."

Mrs. Wakefield looked thoughtful. "Elizabeth," she said slowly, "what you're describing is a very manipulative young lady. Do you think it's possible that Enid has been trying to keep her distance because she's afraid of hurting your feelings?"

"What do you mean?" Elizabeth demanded.

"What I mean," Mrs. Wakefield said, "is that Enid may have sized Amy up much more quickly than you. After all, she wasn't lugging around the same emotional baggage you were. She didn't have all the good memories of Amy that you did, and she didn't feel the same pressure to make things work out."

"So you're saying I was blind to Amy's faults because of our former friendship," Elizabeth mused.

"I think you quite reasonably wanted to give her a chance," Mrs. Wakefield said, smoothing Elizabeth's hair affectionately. "You're a very generous person, and you didn't want to believe your old friend had changed. Especially," she added, smiling, "since Amy's apparently such a pro at making people forgive her."

"So what about Enid?"

Mrs. Wakefield shook her head. "That's hard to say. It's possible Amy treated her one way when you were around and another way when you weren't."

"I thought of that," Elizabeth said, "but I decided Enid would have told me if Amy had ever said or done anything awful to her. Unless—"

"Unless she wanted to spare you," Mrs. Wakefield said gently. "Unless she was afraid that it would put you on the spot if she told you what she really thought."

Suddenly Elizabeth was filled with shame. Enid had been so loyal to her that she had kept her feelings about Amy to herself. And instead of appreciating her kindness, Elizabeth had just worsened the situation. And the night before—

Elizabeth jumped to her feet. "Mom, thank you so much!" she cried. All at once she knew exactly what she wanted to do.

"Where are you going?" Mrs. Wakefield asked, laughing at her daughter's abrupt change in mood.

"Over to Enid's!" Elizabeth cried. "She and I have a lot of talking to do!"

"Drive carefully," her mother called after her.

"I will!" Elizabeth called back. Her heart felt incredibly lighter as she bounded outside toward the car. For the first time in days, even weeks, she knew exactly what she had to do. She just hoped she wasn't too late.

"I just didn't know what to do," Enid confessed, her green eyes brimming with tears as she recollected how terrible she had felt. "I found it really hard to be with Amy, but I was convinced that telling you would be the wrong thing. I didn't want to put you on the spot, Liz. I didn't want you to have to choose between us."

"I was being such an inconsiderate clod, too,"

Elizabeth said. "I could just shake myself! How could I have been so blind?"

"You can't blame yourself," Enid insisted. "You were just being as good-hearted and kind, as you always are, Liz. You wanted to think the best about Amy. And I admired you for it. But—"

"But when she started threatening you," Elizabeth cut in, "telling you not to spend time with me! You should have told me then."

Enid shook her head. "Maybe I should have, Liz. I didn't know what to do. I was so afraid of losing your friendship."

"*You* were!" Elizabeth gasped. "How do you think I felt last night? I almost died!"

Enid grinned. "So did I. I felt like I'd lost my best friend *and* Prince Charming. But all's well that ends well," she added with a giggle. "Chris called this morning. He still wants to go out with me, believe it or not! He said Amy was being a complete pain all the way home, and he couldn't wait to get rid of her. So he's taking me out to dinner tonight," she concluded with a shy smile. "And even more important, you came over to straighten everything out. And, Liz, I'm so glad you did!"

"Me, too," Elizabeth said emphatically. Her eyes shone. "And, Enid, we can really go up to Lake Tahoe this weekend, just as we planned?"

"Of course we can," Enid said warmly. She thought for a moment. "I want you to feel free to invite Amy, too," she said seriously. "Who knows? Maybe after everything that's happened this weekend, she'll be ready for a truce. I'd consider giving her a second chance."

Elizabeth shook her head admiringly. "You," she said warmly, "are the world's nicest, most generous, most caring friend, and I can't even believe my own ears!" She gave Enid an impulsive hug.

"But to be honest," Elizabeth added a moment later, "I don't have much hope that Amy will come along. I hate to admit it, but I'm afraid she really *has* changed. She's not the girl she was a few years ago."

"Well, I guess we all have," Enid said philosophically. "But feel free to invite her anyway. Now that you and I are square with each other again, I feel I can face anything." She grinned. "Even being locked up in a cabin with Amy Sutton for a weekend!"

Elizabeth burst out laughing. She knew exactly what Enid meant. She felt as though she could face anything, too. She had her best friend back. That was all that mattered.

Twelve

An expression of anguish on her face, Jessica burst into the *Oracle* office Monday during study hall. "OK, Liz," she said, frantically searching through the box of letters for Miss Lovelorn on the table. "What happened to those two letters I left in here?"

"What letters?" Elizabeth asked absently.

Jessica looked upset. "Listen to me!" she shrieked. "There were two letters in here. One was signed 'Heartbroken' and the other, 'Missing Her.' I need to find them."

"Oh, *those*," Elizabeth said, sitting up straighter in her chair. "Jess, neither you nor Cara showed up last week to submit copy for your column. And we had to get the paper in to the printer early because we're running a special early edition this week. The paper comes out today. Anyway, you two were nowhere to be found. So I told Penny *I'd* write the column, and I just grabbed—"

Jessica turned pale. "No," she said weakly,

clutching at her heart. "Don't tell me you printed those two letters! You can't do this to me, Liz, not to your own flesh and blood."

Elizabeth stared at her. "Jess, they were the first two I grabbed. I barely even looked at them. I just whipped off a response and handed them to Penny. I should think you'd be grateful to me for keeping your column going," she added. "Otherwise, Penny was going to cut it."

"It doesn't matter," Jessica said mournfully. "Cara and I are finished being Miss Lovelorn anyway. And after those letters come out. . . ." Her voice trailed off miserably. She knew the letters had to be from Jay and Denise. And once they appeared in the paper and they both read them . . .

It was sickening, that's what it was. Jay and Denise were going to make up just from reading Jessica's column. Talk about backfiring!

Well, Jessica thought, she had had it with journalism. And something told her she'd had it with Jay McGuire, too. A glare on her pretty face, she stormed out of the *Oracle* office, slamming the door behind her.

Elizabeth barely noticed her sister's dramatic exit. She was putting the final touches on her "Eyes and Ears" column for the following week's paper. "A handsome prince fell madly in love with a skier at the big bash Saturday," she wrote, smiling a little to herself. There! The column was done. And she had ten minutes left of her study period—time to find Amy Sutton and invite her to come to Lake Tahoe that weekend. She hadn't exchanged a word with Amy since Saturday night, and she had very little idea of what to expect.

A few minutes later she found Amy scribbling furiously in a notebook at one of the tables outside the cafeteria.

"Amy!" Elizabeth called. "Can I join you?"

Amy looked up, a startled expression on her face. "I guess so," she said, shrugging.

"What are you doing?" Elizabeth began, sitting down across from Amy. She really wasn't sure what to say.

Amy raised one eyebrow. "Writing to Johnny," she said flatly. A minute later her face cleared a little. "I don't see why I should be so grouchy with *you*," she admitted at last. "It wasn't your fault that everything got so messed up on Saturday night."

I should say not, Elizabeth thought.

"Actually," Elizabeth said, "I wanted to talk to you about this coming weekend, Amy. How would you like to go skiing, the way we'd planned?"

"Just you and me?" Amy said, looking excited. "I'd really like that."

"Not just you and me," Elizabeth said firmly. "It's Enid's aunt who has the cabin, remember. So it would be the three of us—you, me, and

Enid." She looked directly at Amy. "A chance for a new start, Amy. What do you say?"

Amy looked uncomfortable. "I don't think I really want to come," she said at last. "I'm sorry, Liz. I just can't stand the thought of having to share you with Enid. And Enid"—her brow wrinkled—"just isn't really my idea of fun. You know what I mean?"

"Yes," Elizabeth said, unperturbed. "I know exactly what you mean, Amy."

"Hey, where are you going?" Amy demanded as Elizabeth rose to leave.

Elizabeth smiled gently at her. "I'm sorry, Amy. But I've got class in a few minutes, and I promised Enid I'd find her as soon as possible. We want to give her aunt a firm date this time— and a firm number of how many of us are coming!"

Amy bit her lip. "Are you mad at me?" she asked.

Suddenly Elizabeth felt sorry for Amy. "No," she said truthfully. "I'm not mad at you."

And she really wasn't, she realized as she walked away. Disappointed, yes. And a little hurt, too. Elizabeth had cherished memories of Amy from the sixth grade, and it pained her to admit that her friend had grown up and grown away from her.

No, Elizabeth wasn't mad at Amy. But she couldn't pretend to respect or admire her anymore, either. And she'd never be able to forgive Amy for the way she had treated Enid. She had realized over the last few days how precious Enid's friendship was to her. And Elizabeth knew that whatever happened in the future, she would never do anything to imperil that friendship again.

"It's disgusting, that's what it is," Jessica said to Cara, her aqua eyes blazing as she eyed the couple sitting arm in arm at a table across the crowded cafeteria. "I think I've lost my appetite."

Cara giggled. "I think it's kind of sweet," she objected. "See how happy they look! And to think *our* column actually got them back together."

Jessica put her fingers in her ears. "Stop," she groaned. "I can't bear it!"

But Cara was enjoying herself far too much to stop now. "Listen," she insisted, picking up a copy of *The Oracle* and turning to the center page. " 'Dear Miss Lovelorn,' " she read aloud, ignoring Jessica's pained expression. " 'My boyfriend and I have had a ridiculous misunderstanding. He now believes I think he's too young for me. I don't know what's gone wrong, but I need to prove to him that age doesn't matter. I love him and want him back.' Signed, 'Heartbroken.' "

135

"What does Miss Lovelorn say?" Jessica asked, her curiosity getting the best of her.

"Just 'Read on, the next letter says it all.' " Cara continued, " 'Dear Miss Lovelorn, My girlfriend and I had what must be the stupidest fight in history. Somehow we got it in our heads that the fact that she's a year older than I am really matters. Well, I've decided it doesn't. I've got to make it up to her somehow. The least I can do is let her know, by printing this, that I'm—Missing Her.' "

Jessica pushed her tray away in disgust. "I can't believe my own sister could betray me this way."

"It was your fault." Cara giggled. "*You* were supposed to choose the letters last week, and you forgot!"

"Let's just forget the whole thing," Jessica said moodily. "From the way Jay and Denise are carrying on, it's obvious I'm out of the picture." Her eyes brightened as she watched Cara fold up the paper. "Hey, aren't you excited about the new pledge period?" she demanded.

Cara chuckled. "That's what I love about you, Jess. You always bounce back."

Jessica tossed back her hair. "Well, *I'm* excited." She narrowed her eyes thoughtfully. "I wonder," she said speculatively, watching two girls eating lunch together a few tables away, "why Jeannie West has never been nominated

136

for Pi Beta Alpha. Maybe you should put her up, Cara."

Cara looked surprised. "But Sandy will put her up," she objected. "She's Jeannie's best friend."

Jessica looked intently at the two girls. "Yes," she said finally, pulling her tray back toward her and beginning to eat, "I guess you're right."

"Tuna," Jean West said wearily, looking at her sandwich as though it might bite her. "I really hate sandwiches!"

Sandra took a spoonful of yogurt and said nothing. She wished *she* could eat a sandwich. But she had been gaining weight lately, and unless she starved for the next three weeks, she would burst the seams on her new cheerleading uniform.

"How'd you do on Russo's quiz?" Jean asked, putting her sandwich down. "It was really hard, wasn't it?" Mr. Russo's chemistry quizzes were notorious—and the one they'd been handed back that day was unusually difficult.

"I got an eighty-five," Sandra told her friend. She had actually been pleased with that score. "Why?" she added. "How did *you* do?"

"About the same," Jean said.

"What was your score?" Sandra pressed her.

"Eighty-seven," Jean said. She didn't notice the strange expression on Sandra's face.

It seemed to Sandra lately that Jean was always doing better than she was! Whatever it was, Jean was the one who shone. But Jean was her best friend. They weren't supposed to *compete*. So why did Sandra feel so reluctant to share the only thing she had that Jean didn't?

Pledging season for Pi Beta Alpha was starting in exactly one week. And Sandra knew she was either going to have to put her friend up for membership or risk losing Jeannie forever. And the strange thing was, she still didn't know what she was going to do!

Coming next month, another Super Edition: Jessica and Elizabeth have fun in the sun in **MALIBU SUMMER,** *an extra-big, extra-exciting Sweet Valley High book for your summertime reading.*

Will Sandra nominate Jean for Pi Beta Alpha? And can their friendship last if she doesn't? Find out in Sweet Valley High #30, **JEALOUS LIES,** *available in August.*